COLLISION AT HOME

Callie Sommers

ISBN-13: 9780578907000

Cover design by: Allusion Publishing

Printed in the United States of America

For Melina – Thank you for always listening to the stories that became the stories. This would not have happened without your support and encouragement. For that, I am forever grateful.

Table of Contents

Prologue

The Only Difference Between
Martyrdom and Suicide
Is Press Coverage

~Jayson~

The worst part of a rehab assignment at the minor league affiliate was never the injury itself. These teams had to put in work to get people to come to the games. That meant there was always some sort of promotion or event happening. For me, it meant that I have to take a LOT of pictures and sign tons of baseballs. All that shit is way more work than the actual game. When I am back with the team, I only have to do this stuff occasionally, but here in Fresno, I am the main attraction. Having last year's Silver Slugger in the line-up is a crowd draw. People come to the games to see me. They do back home, too, but not like this. The first night here, people had lined up for hours just for a picture.

Everyone wants a piece of Jayson Martinez. A touch of the fame. I am always careful not to touch them back, though. I wasn't going to put myself in that position. Sure, I fucked around a lot when I was newly single, but that shit got old quick. Too many pro athletes had gotten trapped by some woman who swore she was on the pill or was just fine "with a good time." They never are. All of them want something.

My ex sure wanted it. When I wouldn't put a ring on it after two years, she slept with my teammate. His career was over a year later, and their marriage followed shortly after that. Everyone assumes I get a 'workout' in every town...I don't. It's been a while, and I'm not even going to think about dating until the season is over.

So here I sit in the training room, only partly listening as the operations guy goes over what is happening today. In just over an hour, a bunch of elementary-school kids will be here for some all-star stuff, and then there is a movie on the big screen after our game. It was going to be a long fucking day. The kids were going to get a tour of the stadium, the team's new uniforms are hung in our lockers in the clubhouse, and apparently, they get a pep talk from yours truly. I know I need to talk about hard work and staying in school. That shit always makes me laugh. I was an awful student, and probably one of the laziest guys on my team in high school. Thing is, I can't break these kids' hearts by telling them the truth. You have a one-in-a-million shot at making it, and it doesn't matter how much you love the game, or how hard you work. Either you have "it," or you don't. I was drafted out of high school and only fell back to community college because I deserved a better deal. It took two years, but I got what I wanted from a brand-new team. I am the franchise. This is my tenth year in the league, and I hadn't even thought of slowing down until this last injury.

Obviously, I hadn't been paying much attention until I heard the other guys groan. Apparently, a couple of the kids had a girl for a coach and would need one of the guys on the team to babysit them during the clubhouse stuff. Sucks for those kids and the guy who gets stuck with that job. It must be embarrassing enough to have your mom, or some man-size lady be your coach, but then get a babysitter on top of that? That fucking blows! I was lucky that nobody expected me to volunteer for that job. I would do my part; knock a few balls over the fence, sign some shit, and tell them to stay in school. Then, I'm scheduled for a massage and a nap before the game.

As the team's operations manager, Derrick Martin, wrapped up his little talk and we were leaving to meet the kids, he asked me to come to his office. While I knew this probably meant I got to go home, I still felt like I was getting called to the principal's office.

I flopped down on the big sofa in his office and kicked my foot up on the coffee table. I was waiting for the little folder that had my plane ticket and itinerary in it. It never came. Instead, he went on and on about all the rules of the day and shit I needed to remember. Seriously, I know what I needed to do when the spotlights were on, so I just kept nodding in agreement. However, it was the last bit of his speech that caused me to sit up.

"Whatever you do, Martinez, leave Coach Collins alone. She is a nice person and a great coach. It's hard enough for her being the only female coach out here today, she doesn't need you messing with her." He was being serious, which made poking at him that much more fun. Yeah, I played the part of the arrogant asshole, but that's what it was, an act. Half of my job was to shake hands and kiss babies, and while I hated it, I knew it kept the checks rolling in.

"Look, I'm sure that she is a great gal, which is absolutely code for fucking homely. You don't need to worry about me. I'm sure she is probably more of a pants wearer, anyway, if you get my drift." I got up and walked over to his desk. I picked up a framed picture that looked like a bunch of his friends had taken a boating trip. "Unless she looks like this hot little redhead next to you, I'll leave her alone," I said with a wink. It had to have been his girlfriend in the picture I was pointing to, because he sat up really straight and said, "Just leave her the fuck alone."

Ha! I hit a nerve. It didn't matter because I was just itching to get home. There was really nothing left to say, so I walked out.

Chapter 1

Feels Like Summer

~Cadence~

There is a great sense of memory tied to summer for me. Even at twenty-six, I can close my eyes and smell the chlorine of the pool, the sunscreen, the charcoal grill, the wet sidewalk from sprinklers, the fresh-cut grass, and the damp dirt. Close your eyes and turn your mind off. Take a deep breath. It will all come rushing back. All of it reminds me of a much simpler time. But if I'm being really honest, though, it wasn't simpler back then. It was actually much harder than life is now. Now things are quiet. Now, nobody is gossiping. Maybe that is one of the benefits of getting older. Those things stop, or you just don't care anymore. I'd like to think that after all this time, they have finally stopped.

You are probably thinking the worst right now. Something horrific happened in my childhood that completely ruined summers for me. That's not exactly true. Nothing happened, yet everyone thinks it did, and that's how I earned a reputation that stuck for years. But it wasn't just that summer, it seems like something happened—and continues to happen—every summer that changed or will change my life in some way. I just never know what that moment is until it all comes crashing down.

Growing up in a town of less than fifteen-thousand people has its advantages. There is a certain feeling of security in knowing just about everyone in your town. But therein lies the problem...you know everyone, and everyone knows you and your business. If they aren't related to you by blood or marriage, they are your neighbor, and even then, you are often somehow related to your neighbor. The parents of the kids I went to school with went to school with my parents. The entire community is one giant game of telephone where people actually believe what they hear on the other line, no questions asked. We didn't have or even need social media back then, the gossip mill made sure everyone knew your business all the time.

The summer after I started high school, I had one of those awkward, teenage make-out sessions that ended well before any reproductive parts were exposed. Of course, that isn't the story that was told. I don't think I was home for an hour before my best friend at the time called asking me how it felt to finally lose my virginity. Wait, what? I had absolutely no idea what she was talking about. It was like that part in *Ferris Bueller's Day Off* where Ferris's classmate said, "My best friend's sister's boyfriend's brother's girlfriend heard from this guy who knows this kid that..." You get the idea. Less than an hour after my first real kiss, I was the town tramp. There was no defending or refuting. The first story out was always the truth, no matter if there were facts backing it up or not. Hearing this from Christina wasn't the worst of it. I knew it was only a matter of time before my mother heard. I would face that horror before the day was done, and while she ended up believing me, the damage had been done. My mom and I were extremely close, and I never wanted to let her down. I think this hurt her, and that fact crushed me. I only ever wanted to make my mom proud. When I was too little to remember, my dad left us. She took on the responsibilities of being both parents. My grandparents were a big help, but it was really all her. Both of my sisters were older than me by eight and ten years, so I didn't develop the sister bond that they had. It was just me and Mom, and now it was me and her and this horrible rumor.

By the time school started a few weeks later, everyone knew. Nate got high fives in the hall, and I took the long way to class. I retreated further into the safe zone I had created. I cut everyone out. The people whom I had been friends with since first grade were now strangers. Sadly, I was just fine with that fact. If they didn't believe me, they weren't my friends anyway. That's pretty much how the next three years of my life went. I was easy fodder for the next person who wanted to claim a notch in their bedpost. Every now and then I would let my guard down enough to let someone take me out, only to end up fighting them off at the end of the night. Each of those times only added to the layer of ice that I developed around my heart. Being cold and shut off was the way I would make it to the other side. I knew I just had to endure until it was time to graduate. I knew I wouldn't have to deal with them or the constant gossip forever. I had already decided that I needed to get away as soon almost immediately after I was handed my diploma as possible.

I worked my ass off. I took every advanced class that was offered, and even took community college classes that would count toward my high school diploma too. I also spent my time in the gym. I played basketball, worked out, practiced ju-jitsu, and even took dance classes. I made sure I was too busy to deal with the constant buzz of my small town. Having everyone talking about you all the time is no way to live. I didn't go to the cool parties, and I didn't go to the school dances. My sole focus was on getting out and starting over. But just five days before I crossed the stage for my diploma, on the weekend signaling the official start of summer, my life changed again. I never got to take the stage to get my diploma, but at least I got to graduate.

Despite my mom wanting to keep me close after everything that had happened, I had earned my place at the University of Nevada, Las Vegas, and I was going to take it. I moved into the dorms knowing I was going to have to put up with a roommate I didn't know. The only thing that really worried me was whether or not my new roommate was the kind who would bring a new person back to the dorm every night. I didn't want my dorm room to have a revolving door. All the bad shit I went through over the years must have paid off, because literally the first thing Cecily ever said to me was, "I don't care who or what you choose to do, you don't bring that shit here. This is our sanctuary, our place to escape all the crazy of this town, and I don't want to memorize some elaborate scrunchie system just to be able to enjoy my home." I laughed out loud in a way that let her know that not only was I relieved, but that she had a new friend who also needed exactly that kind of peace. She has been my absolute best friend from that moment on. We were both California girls, but she had more of the stereotypical Cali life than me. Cecily grew up at the beach in southern California, and I grew up in the middle of orchards and vineyards. She was ridiculously tall with olive skin and dark hair, while I was average in just about every way possible. I wasn't overly tall or incredibly thin. I was generally pale, which went with my red hair, and I didn't even come by that naturally. It had, however, been some shade of ginger since my mom allowed me to dye it when I was fourteen. I suppose the only thing really unique about me were my eyes, which were multi-tonal. They were generally blue with yellow and orange halos in the middle. They actually looked like they changed colors depending on what I wore. Other than our outward appearances, we shared so much in common. Music, movies, food, all of it. She was the best friend I had been missing. Luckily, we had the same major and we both wanted to work with kids. She was two years older than me, though, but I was starting school as a second semester sophomore because of all the classes I took back home. Because I was so far ahead, we were able to take many of our classes together. I was able to help her keep up when she traveled with the volleyball team, and she let me have a break from the day-to-day school grind during her off season. College really became a game changer for me. I was finally free of the shit that had weighed me down.

After graduation, Cecily and I decided to move back to California to get started on life. She didn't have any ties to her home town after her parents decided to retire and travel. My mom was home and retired, so I thought it would be nice to be close to her. Going home was going to be hard, but it was time. There were tons of jobs waiting for us when we were done, and even though we didn't follow the exact same career path, we remained roommates for four years. About a year ago Cecily had saved up enough to buy her own place. It was time for both of us to spread our wings a bit more.

Around that same time my mom had decided that she wanted a smaller place, so I bought my childhood home from her and began to renovate it. I kept the extent of my project pretty low-key. Cecily was excited about her new place, and I didn't want to take anything away from her hard work and excitement. I helped her move and have a housewarming party. She did the same for me a few months later. Of course, when she saw my place, she was a little surprised. She had been to my house plenty of times while we were in school, but it wasn't the same outdated, split-level it had once been. Everything in my house had been updated. From the flooring to the fixtures, I had done a complete renovation. Even the pool and landscaping changed. I wanted to make this place my forever home, so I did exactly what I wanted to do my whole life. I explained it away with, "Things are a lot less expensive here in a small town, and my mom sold me the house for next to nothing." It wasn't the whole truth, but she never pressed me on it.

I was back living in the same town that had almost crushed me years earlier. While I loved my home, I did everything I could to keep my life as private as I could. I wasn't about to be the gossip that would now spread among the mom gang that was comprised of my former classmates. I didn't shop here, and I only ate at a few restaurants. I made sure to keep my private life private.

I work as an intervention counselor in a rural school almost thirty miles from my house. I love the long, quiet drive at the end of the day as much as I love my job. I see kids and their families when they are at their lowest points. Poor attendance, bad grades, and fighting are just symptoms. All of those things are masks for deeper issues like home instability, poverty, and even learning disabilities. I learned very early on that the kids that need the most love and compassion ask for it in the most difficult ways.

Since the school I work for is so small, all staff are required to take on an extra duty like coaching a sport or supervising a club. With my background, sports was the obvious choice. Coaching also helps me keep the kids that I see in the fold. They could make friends and have goals to work towards. Strictly by chance, baseball was the sport that was available when adjunct duties were up for grabs. And while I had once loved basketball, baseball was in my blood. I used to play catch with my grandpa all the time. He loved this game more than anything, and he taught me to love it too.

While I know elementary school is about learning and not about winning, winning is awesome, and I am incredibly competitive. I also secretly relish the looks on the male coaches' faces when they get bested by a girl. But now it's summer vacation, and I only have one more school obligation left. Then I can have some fun and let go of being Miss/Coach Collins and just be Cadie.

Chapter 2

Boys of Summer

I'm sitting in the outfield of our local AAA ballpark. It's mid-June, so at eight at night it's only now starting to get dark. After some of the games, they show a movie on the big scoreboard. These are the fun things that happen in the minor leagues. There are families scattered all over the grass. While I am not technically alone, I am not here with family, and none of my friends wanted to sit in the heat. Instead, they are a few blocks away at the brewery where I will be shortly. I sit just a few feet from the families of the boys on my team. A couple of the players on my baseball team got to play in the game today that the local affiliate hosted. Since I am a winning coach, I got to be on the field with my team. But let's be honest, I never got to coach. I didn't even get to step foot in the clubhouse. I understand why, but it did further force the separation. The men did their thing, and I kept to myself. Even though I am five years in, they don't trust that I know what I'm doing. I keep winning, and I keep getting questioned. That's how it has always been. It doesn't bother me anymore. Well, it does, but they will never know.

When we arrived earlier today, I was immediately left out of the main activities for the first hour or so. I handed my players off to the care of a benchwarmer since a woman in the locker room just can't happen. I busied myself out on the field with the help of my brother-in-law. He works with the AAA team as a hitting coach. I leaned on him for a lot of help, and he was always happy to rope other coaches in as well. Since I had time to kill, I figured I could hit some balls. Phillip happily stood behind the screen and threw to me for almost the whole hour. After a few swings with an aluminum bat we have to use, Phil convinced me to hit with wood like the big boys do. There is no better sound than a wooden bat making good contact. I was pretty pleased that I was able to hit a few good ones. The boys were going to come out soon, so Phillip and I collected the mess of balls I hit. This was a good warm-up for him since he was the one who was going to have to throw for the hitting contest that was up first.

I leaned forward on the rail of the first base dugout giving one last bit of hitting advice to Davis. A few seconds later I heard the loud ping and watched the ball go right over the temporary wall they had put up. The pride that bubbled up inside quickly turned to shock when I felt a finger trace up the back of my leg from my ankle to the hem of my shorts and heard a deep voice say, "If you had been my hitting coach when I was his age, I would have never skipped practice. Hell, even now I'd show up early for you." I turned, not thinking of trying to hide the blush that I knew had overcome me, only to be face to face with none other than Jayson Martinez. He casually stepped back to lean on the door to the clubhouse, smiling in a way that he knew melted the panties right off the ladies. To say Jayson was handsome was an understatement. His skin was tan, his eyes were a rich cognac color, and his overlong hair was jet black. A well-chiseled jaw boasted a five o'clock shadow. He was cocky, and when he saw I was ruffled, he laughed.

I quickly retorted, "Maybe if you would listen to your coaches, you wouldn't have to be here dealing with the peasants while you rehab."

A few weeks earlier there had been a very scary collision at home plate, and Jayson hurt his back and hit his head pretty hard. He was one of the most powerful catchers in the league, a Silver Slugger. Jayson was a wall, way bigger than most catchers at six-two. He was powerful with huge shoulders and biceps. Also doing squats for a living created an ass that you could bounce a quarter off of. Why did I know this, and why did I care? I had to walk away, I had to make some space. I quickly took the steps onto the field to get away from him, but I could feel his gaze burn into my back. I also heard the laugh that escaped him as I walked away.

The rest of the day was a blur, there were trophies and celebrations. Of course, my boys had placed first and second, respectively, in hitting, and I was on cloud nine. So here I sit, flipping through my phone, deciding on whether I needed to text a distraction to meet up with later when I get an AirDrop notification. I didn't recognize the name, *I. Ketcher*, so I declined it because I wasn't interested in opening a random dick pic. Whoever it was had to be close or it wouldn't have gone though, so I started to look around. That's when I saw him again. He was leaning against the short wall of the field. It looked as though he had already showered and changed from the game. He was wearing tan cargo shorts and a light blue V-neck tee that had sleeves stretched very tight. He was looking directly at me as he tapped his phone again. Instantly, my phone pinged with the same notification. I accepted and read the message that accompanied his contact:

Ketcher: I hope this is the phone of the beautiful Coach Collins. Maybe a private hitting lesson sometime?

Great, I'm sure that's how he gets them. "Here's my burner number, hit me up so I have something to brag about tomorrow in the locker room." That was pretty much my reply. I rose quickly and bid my farewells to my players and their families. I couldn't stay for the movie. I needed a shower and a drink. I also needed something else, but that could be figured out later.

Chapter 3

Sweater Weather

I made it home in less than fifteen minutes, when it usually took twice that long. For some reason I spent much longer than I needed to getting ready to head back out. I had to wash the day off of me. Out of habit, I ran a razor over my legs. I had spent a good amount of money on laser hair removal, so it was a moot point, but habit, nonetheless. I tried on too many outfits, and even fussed over my stupid tan lines when I finally settled on a pair of high-waisted shorts and a black tank that had a skull cut out in the back. Spending the last few months coaching had left me with the most ridiculous tan lines ever. It basically looked like I got a spray tan while wearing low-cut socks and a t-shirt. I could hide the ankles with a cute, strappy shoe, the tank didn't hide anything. It was much too hot for anything else, and I guess I really didn't care. I wasn't going out to impress anyone. Except in the back of my mind, I was. I swear I could still feel his finger travel up the back of my leg. There is no way Jayson Martinez would be at a local bar, so I shook that thought out of my head. I wasn't going to see him again.

While I was buckling my wedge sandals, my phone rang, and I started to laugh. If I didn't immediately text Cecily back, she would call me. Seriously, I usually had less than a minute to reply before my phone rang. I had just heard a text and knowing I had missed a few texts while getting dressed, I picked up without looking at the screen and immediately said, "I know I'm running behind Ceci, but I'll meet you on the patio in twenty minutes. You are still at The C, Right?"

A baritone voice that sent a shiver down my spine replied, "I've never not had to ask someone out for a drink before they agree to go. I'll see you there!" Before I got the chance to say anything else, the call disconnected. I looked down at my phone knowing exactly who had called, but I still needed affirmation. I scrolled through the texts I got while I was in the shower. None of them had come from my best friend. They were all from him.

Jayson: Just so you know, whatever I choose to do and with whom I do it, isn't anyone's business. I'm not who everyone thinks I am.

Jayson: I was dead serious when I said that if you were my coach, I'd never be late to practice.

Jayson: You are incredibly sexy, and the fact that you know baseball is really just an incredible bonus on top of the prize of a lifetime.

Holy shit! Who says stuff like that? I didn't even know this guy, except for what you see in the tabloids and on SportsCenter. There were always pictures of new women draped all over him with sordid tales that matched the visuals. Not only was I not that girl, I never wanted to be that girl. I was happy just living a very quiet life; having everyone speculate about my sex life wasn't something I ever wanted to entertain again.

I typed out a text to my best friend and I drove as fast as I could to try and get my friends to change venues. The lack of replies, or even texts, meant that they were already far past the point of bar hopping for the evening. It was a good thing I decided to bring the Escalade tonight, since I was more than certain I'd be driving their drunk asses home.

By the time I got to the bar, the big crowd was already spilling out on the patio, but that wasn't all that unusual for a Saturday night. I had to text Ceci to find out exactly where she was sitting. Again, no response, but I knew as soon as I stepped all the way out of the main bar that there must be something worth clamoring over in the corner. I grabbed my one drink before making my way through the crowd.

Finally able to get close enough to get Cecily's attention, she waved me though the mass of strangers. "Why didn't you mention that your friend Jayson was joining us tonight?" Ceci questioned?

I can only assume that he was sitting there with my friends because of Derrick. There was no other way for him to know who I would be with. That wasn't what came out of my mouth, though. I shot back at her, "If you would have answered your phone you would have, and he wouldn't have. I also don't even know him well enough to call him a friend."

Dramatically clutching his chest as if I had wounded him, he said, "Now, Coach Collins, I've been nothing but complimentary to you today. You could at least let me help your friends celebrate your victories." I rolled my eyes as all of my friends erupted in toasts and cheers. I was really lucky that I had a group of friends who didn't judge and were always supportive. They were absolutely going to roast me later, but for now they just let it go.

The evening went exactly how I thought it would, considering the celebrity at our table. People were just hanging around for no reason, just to listen. They asked for pictures and autographs. This wasn't fun or relaxing for me. I was quiet for much of the night, mostly because I wasn't able to even get a word in. It was nearing one in the morning when Jayson looked over at Derrick and said, "This is so stupid, man. Can't you do something so that I can at least talk to Coach Collins here? I haven't been able to speak two words without being interrupted."

Before Derrick even opened his mouth, I basically shouted, "Maybe she doesn't want to talk to you!" Ceci grabbed my arm just and gave me the look that warned of the extra attention surrounding us.

It was all getting to be a little too much, so I excused myself to the ladies' room. It was more of an excuse for some air, than the need to pee. Right as my hand hit the ladies' room door, there was a tug on my elbow. I half expected to see some drunk in desperate need of the facilities, but instead it was Derrick. We hadn't been friends for long, but over the past year he had made his way into my small circle. I met him at a fundraiser for the team that we had played with earlier that day. He worked in the main office, having something to do with operations. Maybe that was one of the reasons he showed up tonight. Was he the handler for the superstar bad boy? Derrick was a good guy, and while I think his interest was more than friendship, it just wasn't there. I stayed away from relationships, and even further away from anything involving those in my circle of friends. That's why what he said next was a bit of advice that was too familiar to come from a new friend.

"Cadie, whatever you do, please do not fuck Jayson. He is nothing but bad news. Just stay away from him." I could tell that this was the drunken truth of a friend who would feel bad about it tomorrow, if he even remembered it.

"Now, Derrick, you should have learned by now that who I choose to 'fuck', as you so politely put it, is really only the business of the two people doing the fucking. I appreciate your input, as misguided as it may be. But you are way out of line." I could feel the anger bubbling up, and in an attempt to keep from saying something very hurtful to him, I stepped inside the ladies' room.

He was gone by the time I exited, and for me the night was also over. I was hoping I would be able to wrangle my friends into the car and get everyone home without much of a fight. They were all pretty well sauced, so it was probably going to be about as easy as giving a cat a bath.

I made my way back to the table and saw that they were all taking that last, long drink before they headed out. Wow, they were making this easy on me! Looking at the group, there were six when there had been five, and two of the faces I didn't know. Derrick was gone, and he had been replaced by a couple of very drunk college girls who I am sure were ready to do just about anything to go home with Jayson. I asked Cecily where Derrick went, and she let me know that he shoved off just a few minutes ago after calling for a ride.

We walked toward the exit, and when we got to the street I lied and said I only had room for three in my car. The rest would need to find their own way home. This way I wouldn't have to deal with watching Jayson take Blonde One and Blonde Two back to their sorority house. To my shocked surprise, Jayson said, "Actually, I'm the only one who needs a lift, my ride took off already." I guess that is why Derrick showed up tonight.

Ceci looked at me with her sideways smile and gave me a wink, "We went ahead and called for an Uber so you wouldn't have to go out of your way."

There were still a couple people I wasn't interested in dealing with and she knew it. In her very best bitch voice, she said, "They aren't smart enough to figure out that they aren't part of this carpool equation. You are going to have to be a bit more direct if you aren't going to be giving them a *ride*." She wasn't talking to me; she was staring dead at Jayson.

He let out a throaty laugh and said, "I'm sorry, I was so transfixed with Coach Collins here that I hadn't realized that we had been followed."

He turned toward them and said, "Ladies, I appreciate your support, and I am more than happy to sign something or pose for a picture, but I really need to get going home with my friends." It was almost as if their boobs deflated right along with their egos, but not enough to pose for one more picture. Blonde One shoved her phone at me, and Jayson crossed his arms over his chest. They took hold of either bicep, then got on their toes trying to kiss him on the cheeks. He smiled wide for the picture and thanked them again for supporting the team. I made sure the photo wasn't flattering for either of them. Not even sure why I was being petty, he had effectively dismissed them for us. They sulked off in typical fashion, with cutting remarks about each of us girls who were left. Cecily looked down at her phone to confirm that the car at the curb was their ride. It was, so I hugged each of my friends goodbye promising to come help them retrieve their cars tomorrow.

"Okay, let's go. I'm sure you broke all kinds of curfew rules. I'd better get you home." As soon as it was out of my mouth, I realized just how annoyed I sounded. I wasn't annoyed with the task of driving him home, I was just upset about my not-relaxing night out.

Before I could even get out my apology, Jayson said, "You really do sound like a coach. And I don't have a curfew. And I don't want to go home yet."

Surprised by his comments, I asked in a mocking tone, "Well, if you aren't interested in going home, Mr. Martinez, where exactly would you like to go?"

He gave me a questioning look and shrugged his shoulders. "I don't really know what goes on around here, and I don't really want to be around a bunch of people. I'd like to be able to talk to you without being interrupted. We can go to my apartment, or yours, if you are more comfortable. Do you have roommates who would be bothered?"

So, superstar wants to "talk" alone?

"No, I don't have roommates, and no, we aren't going to my place to be alone. I don't do that. The only things open are those twenty-four-hour diners, and I can pretty much guarantee that you will be accosted by the same kinds of people who just spilled out of the bar we were in." He wasn't interested in that option, and for some reason I can't seem to comprehend, I offered up a place that I knew would be quiet and would also have the peace I needed to clear my own upset thoughts.

"There is a beach not far from my place, and I can guarantee there aren't going to be people there right now."

Looking very confused, Jayson asked, "A beach? In the middle of California? You aren't going to drive me hours away and then dump my body in a ditch somewhere, are you?" He couldn't even get the last part out without laughing.

"No, Jayson, it's not too far away, and I would need at least one other person to move the body. You have over one-hundred pounds and probably six inches on me, so at the very least, I'd need to have the hole already dug. Since it's just me and you, you can assume that you are safe." I motioned for him to follow me down to the end of the street toward my SUV. He followed but looked past my truck for what I could only assume would be a small sedan. I could see the look of surprise on his face when I beeped the alarm on the Escalade at the curb.

"Won't your boyfriend be upset that you are driving another man around in his truck?" he asked.

The bitchy annoyance came right back out of my mouth when I said, "Surely any man who I date would not be that insecure."

"So, he won't be upset?" he asked in an attempt to get more information from me.

Knowing that his reason for asking, and waiting for him to just get out and ask it, I simply replied, "No."

I could see him deflate just a little before he finally said, "So, no, as in no boyfriend, or no, he won't be upset?"

I answered his question by saying, "Cadillac actually allows the sale of these vehicles to women. I am also very much single with no interest in dating. Now, are you ready to finally get out of here?" Talking at the same time I was walking, I reached for the driver's side door. Jayson quickly grabbed it and opened it. "Oh no, I'm the only one who drives," I said just as I realized that I was now enclosed in

Jayson's massive frame. One of his hands was on the handle, and the other was up on the doorjamb.

He smiled down at me, "And just because you are a strong, independent woman doesn't mean a guy can't be a gentleman and open the door for you." Closing my eyes at the admonishment, I took in a deep breath, inhaling that overtly man scent of sandalwood and spice. I'm fairly certain I let out an audible moan. Quickly, I hopped in and waited for Jayson to get in and buckle up before I started the car and drove off toward my own private heaven.

Chapter 4

Broken Bridge

Almost immediately, my phone connected to the Bluetooth and the music came on very loud. I had a habit of turning it up too loud when I was rushing, as if the loud music made me drive faster. Strangely enough, I think it did. I started to turn it down so any conversation could be heard between us too. As fast as I turned it down, Jayson turned it up, choosing to shout over the music instead. "A person's choice in music can tell a LOT about them. So, tell me, Coach Collins, what do you call this playlist, and what am I going to learn about you?" I thought about it for a minute before I responded. "I can't say you will learn too much about me from this one. It's all just songs about summer here in California."

He raised an eyebrow as if he were studying me and said, "I think that says way more about you than you think it does."

My reply once again came too quickly out of my mouth, "You don't know the first thing about me. And to be honest, I don't even know why you are feigning to care."

"That says a lot about you too. But I know more than you think I do. I now know Coach Collins is very closed off and doesn't think too highly of herself. I just haven't figured out why," he said in a frank tone that sounded way too much like all the therapists I've talked to over the years. With another deep breath and roll of my neck that was a clear signal for him to drop the subject, Jayson sat quietly for a few minutes before he started in with questions about where we were going and how we were going to get to the beach if we were driving toward the mountains. I politely explained that we were in the Central Valley, and therefore surrounded by mountains, and no matter what beach we were headed to, we would need to go toward mountains to get to our destination. My very elementary school answer wasn't satisfactory, and if I didn't know better, I think I could sense a bit of nervousness. Just because I was in a bit of an ornery mood, I played a little more. "Maybe you shouldn't get into SUVs with strange women if you are this scared. Certainly, you aren't actually frightened of me." I was almost cackling as the last bit came out. Knowing now that I was only joking, he relaxed and leaned his head back.

He took a few deep breaths in before he said, "You have absolutely no idea how nice it is to just drive in peace." Actually, I did because the drive home every day I made in complete silence. It was the best way to relax before I got home. I decided to give him some peace, and the next twenty minutes were driven with only the road noise and music playing in the background.

When we pulled off the road onto the gravel drive, Jayson opened his eyes. Out here it was very dark. There wasn't any light from the city, and so the path was only illuminated by my headlights. We got to the closed gate and he looked a little pissed. "We seriously drove all this way and it's closed? That wasn't something you checked ahead of time?"

"Oh yes, Jayson, it was my plan all day to lure you out here to a closed beach," I said with a bit of an eyeroll. "Shit, I didn't even know we were coming here until half an hour ago! And before you get even more upset for absolutely no reason, I have a key to the gate."

Jayson quickly apologized and hopped out of my truck. I could see him jog around the front to get my door, so I let him. "See, this strong, independent woman can accept a gentlemanly gesture."

"I guess it's a good thing you still think I'm a gentleman. I'm afraid you won't think so when I ask you to make that same little moan you made when we were leaving. It was very hot!" he said it with a bit of a laugh. I knew my face was bright red. My only reprieve was that it was dark, and the inside light was behind me, so I know my face wasn't easy to make out.

I stepped down and made my way to the back to get some blankets and some lavender oil to keep the mosquitos at bay. As the hatch lifted, I felt the change in the air when Jayson spotted the jogging stroller that was in the back, along with some blankets. I didn't offer any explanation. If he didn't ask, I wasn't going to say anything. It wasn't like I had anything to hide from him, and to be honest, I really enjoyed watching him squirm. I handed over a couple of blankets and began digging around in my bag for the mosquito repellant. Pulling out a few vials, I unscrewed the cap and asked Jayson for his arm. I rolled a little on his wrist, and then grabbed the other. I made a few more swipes on his neck and ankles before I switched over the lavender for myself. He watched closely as I worked, never taking his eyes off me. I quickly changed out of my wedge sandals to some cheap flip flops that were perfect for the water and the beach. I pressed the button to close the hatch and started over toward the fence. Jayson followed behind with the arm load of blankets. I unlocked the small gate and let him in. He waited for me as I closed it behind me. Since it was pretty dark, I turned on the flashlight on my phone and grabbed his elbow.

We made our way down the short walk to the water. Obviously, we weren't at the ocean, and the beach was a bit rocky, but it would smooth out, and there was sand near the water. I took the blankets from his arms and laid one down on the shore. Jayson strolled over to the water, and just as he reached a hand down, I said, "It's a lot colder and a lot faster than it looks. Don't go stripping down and jumping in." His fingers touched the water and he pulled them back quickly.

"Holy shit! It's like ice water."

"Well, it pretty much is," I replied. "See, all the water in this river is from the winter snow in those mountains right there. Melted snow tends to be pretty cold." I was sounding very bitchy, and I wasn't sure why my temper was so short. I was so off balance. Everything that was happening was so far from what I normally did. I always made plans, and someone always knew where I was. Tonight, as soon as we left the bar, I was on my own. I had made jokes about murdering him. Why didn't I think he could do the same? Not the jokes, but the actual murder part. I suppose the fact that he would need my vehicle to escape was the only thing keeping me safe. Deep down I knew that wasn't true, but it still crossed my mind. I need to quit watching all those murder shows.

I was sitting on the blanket hugging my knees, looking at the water and so engrossed in my own thoughts that I didn't even realize that Jayson sat next to me until he was basically touching my hip.

"I can see why you come out here to relax," he said very quietly. "It's so peaceful and dark. You can really just let your mind clear. No distractions, just white noise."

The only thing I could squeak out was, "Exactly."

"You drove a complete stranger to your private thinking spot. I have to know why. What is going on in that beautiful head of yours, Coach Collins? Who are you?" He had sure packed a lot of questions in just a couple of lines. None of the answers I had could be that brief. Everything he asked of me was some long, drawn-out answer that very few people had heard before. I wasn't exactly sure if it was anything that I was ready to share. At the same time, I'll probably never see him after this, and it was easy to say things to strangers you knew couldn't hold it against you later. Not having a clue as to where to start, I asked him exactly what he wanted to know because what he asked was too broad and vague.

"Just tell me a little about yourself first. You know, the resume version" he clarified. "I'll ask follow-ups for the good stuff."

"Let's see. Name is Cadence Collins and I am twenty-six years old. I've worked in a school and been a coach for five years now. Before that, I was a student at the University of Nevada, Las Vegas. I grew up in that little town you see right over there." I pointed to the lights you could see in the distance just behind us. "I think that is the brief resume version. Unless you want to know my typing speed and computer skills," I said with a smile.

"At least we are getting somewhere now. What do you do at the school you work for, and why go to Nevada if you grew up here? There have to be some good schools closer to home." Jayson was being inquisitive, and if I didn't know better, I would think he was actually interested.

"I work as in intervention counselor. Basically, I help out kids and their families that are in need of support. So not quite a teacher and not quite a social worker." I had actually earned my teaching credential, I just wasn't exactly using it.

"As for why I went to Nevada, that is a little complicated and also very simple. I got a scholarship. I also got the opportunity to get away. Small towns can be a bit stifling. Things didn't turn out exactly as planned, but I can say now they turned out exactly how they were supposed to."

"That was a good half answer, Coach Collins. I have a feeling there is a lot more to the story than you are telling me." His brow was a bit furrowed, but he was smiling. "Getting a scholarship to go to school out of state must mean you are one of those crazy geniuses. Or a resume packer who was involved in every school activity available."

I let out a long sigh and said, "Neither of those things are true. Okay, I will admit that I am smart. Just not in the innovative, genius, full-ride-to-the-Ivy-League kind of way. I had to work for good grades in my classes. And I was so far removed from being involved in school activities that you would be hard pressed to find me in my high school yearbook beyond the obligatory student picture. I did, however, play basketball outside of school, and it afforded me a few opportunities that would have otherwise been out of reach." That last part was really hard to say. It was just something I never really talked about. Sensing my discomfort in the last few words, Jayson reached his hand to my back in an attempt to comfort me.

As soon as I felt his hand touch my skin, I sat straight. First, even years after the accident there was still a nerve in my back that was sensitive to the touch. Second, I had a couple very large scars that I kept hidden from just about everyone. Third, Jayson's touch was so much more. It was real, it was kind, it was comforting. It was going to get me hurt. At first, he pulled back, but almost immediately he returned. His thumb brushed lightly over the shorter horizontal scar. This one was more raised. The much longer vertical one was perceptible but not nearly as pronounced. I knew he couldn't see them, but he could feel them. He already knew the answer when he questioned, "Is this why you don't play anymore?" I nodded slowly. "I take it you don't really like to talk about it." Again, a very slow nod. "You don't have to say anything you don't want to. It's obviously personal, but I'd love to hear about it. I think it will help me to know you more." He couldn't possibly mean that. Really, why was he so interested? He didn't even know me. I guess he was trying, and the fact that he sounded like he cared allowed me to spill the story out to only the third person in my entire life. He sat quiet with his arm wrapped around my shoulder as I first recalled the "deflowering" story that started the gossip. The story that basically everyone already knew. Then I told him the story about the crash that changed my entire life.

I had been driving home late one night, which was actually early in the morning, when I was hit by a drunk driver. My travel basketball team played in a town in the

South Valley, and I did quite a bit of my own driving to get me to games and practices since my mom worked and didn't really have time to haul me all over. I had stayed late in the gym that night trying desperately to hit my twenty-straight free throws. I did that at the end of every practice. I forced myself to hit twenty in a row before I left. Miss one and start over. That night it took longer than usual. Knowing I had a nearly two-hour drive home, one of my teammates offered to let me stay with her, but I had to work at the community center at 9 AM. I got myself in the car and drove. Only fifteen more minutes and I would have been home in bed. This was always the most difficult part of the drive. It was mostly just a straight shot north on the freeway, then I turned off and it was back country roads. I had driven this route hundreds of times. It was second nature to me. I guess I should have been more cautious. I should have taken one more look. I had stopped at the four-way and was almost all the way through the intersection when I was hit. I didn't even see them coming. Their headlights weren't on. They ran the stop sign. It was over in seconds, but the chaos lasted a lot longer. I was hit on the passenger side and my head hit the window. That pain I understood, what I didn't understand was why my legs were going numb. The rest was a blur. I remember the firefighters covering me with a blanket as they used some equipment to break my door open. I remember looking up at the roof of the ambulance. I remember the loud siren. I remember hearing "One DOA." Someone had died in this crash. Then, it was evening, and I was lying flat on my back looking up at fluorescent lights.

"I was taken to the hospital because my back was broken, among other things. I had to have two vertebrae fused together and lots of stitches. I was a mess of purple and blue. I could, however, feel my legs again. They did everything right. It could have been way worse. And for my classmate, it was. He was arrested for driving under the influence and vehicular manslaughter. The girl he had in the passenger seat wasn't wearing her seatbelt and didn't make it." By the time I was finished, tears had started falling. I hadn't cried about this in years. I hadn't talked about it in years either, but that didn't mean I didn't think about it every fucking day. Jayson just sat there and listened and squeezed my shoulder. We sat quietly for what could have been a few minutes or an hour, I couldn't tell. I wiped my face with my palms and then on the blanket.

"Can you tell me what happened after that?" Jayson was cautious in his wording. I knew he wanted to know what happened to my classmate, but I think he also wanted to know what happened to me. "I spent the summer in rehab so that I could go away to college without my walker. There is no sexy way to have a walker in Vegas," I joked. "Nate pleaded guilty to the charges and got a reduced sentence. He was out in three years since he was a minor when it happened. But he has to live with what he did. After he was released, he disappeared. They had to tell me he got out, but not where he went. To be honest, I don't really care. I survived. I feel bad for the family of the girl he killed. She isn't coming back."

Jayson had a very surprised look on his face when I turned to look at him. "Hold on, you said Nate. As in the same guy who spread the sex rumor about you. Like if that would have never happened, you wouldn't have been playing ball so far away and then never been on that road?" He had been listening. Like he really had taken in everything I had said during my meltdown. It was almost as if he was angry. He had dropped his hand from my shoulder and ran it through his hair.

"I guess so, I never really thought about it that way," I said with a shrug.

"How are you not fucking furious or a mental case?" he shouted.

"Being upset about it wasn't going to change the outcome, and there is a very good possibility that I am mental. I did drive a stranger out to the river in the middle of the night." I was trying to make light of the situation, but he wasn't having it.

Resigned, I shrugged again and said, "I could walk, though I couldn't play basketball again. More importantly, I was alive and getting out." The university and my coaches were incredible. They had offered to let me stay on as a scholarship athlete, but I didn't feel right taking the spot of someone who could actually play. My family actually had the means to pay for me to be there, so I went. "The only thing I was upset about was that my mom still had to live here, and people in this town don't let that stuff go. She had to deal with it for a lot longer than I did, kind of like the whole deflowering story. I only just moved back home because my mom retired, and I was able to buy my childhood home from her. I mean, I've been back in the valley for a few years, but I stayed in the city. My body is much different now that I'm not playing basketball all day, and go by Cadie and not Cadence, so I don't think people connect the dots. I also do everything in my power to fly under the radar, so people leave me alone. I stay off social media, so it's hard to know if those people even know I'm around." For me it was simple, but I saw the wheels turning in Jayson's eyes.

"Was that one of those traumatic events that has you swearing off men forever?" He wasn't asking, but he was asking.

"No, Jayson, I lost my virginity a long time ago. But I do still have the box it came in," I said with a little wink. He laughed almost immediately.

"I do, however, conduct myself a bit more carefully these days. You know, simple things like don't bring men around your friends or family if it isn't serious, only accept dates made verbally, never take a call after 9 PM from a man, never accept a weekend date after Wednesday. I know now it is silly, but it works." If I'm being honest, though, I don't really date per se. And I can't even think of any guy who has met my family in a non-platonic way.

"I could see why some might think all the rules are a bit much, but I can also understand. Coach Cadie protects her heart and it is very sweet. I guess I am very lucky that you didn't know it was me calling earlier. How did you not know? You had my number." I let him in on Cecily's habit of calling me if I don't immediately answer her texts, and then I overshared that there wasn't any man who would be calling me anyway. That got me a raised brow and a smile. "Since it's already the weekend, I suppose you won't have dinner with me tomorrow. So how about Monday? It's not the weekend, and you didn't say anything about weekday dates." There was an uptick of hope in his voice.

I smiled back, "I suppose you are right. I can accept a Monday date. But I will still see you tomorrow."

"You are going to break the rules for me?" He looked both surprised and intrigued.

"No, I'm not breaking the rules for you, I'm a season ticket holder."

Jayson then asked with an undertone of hope, "Will you see me after the game?"

"Probably not, my date probably won't make it through the game since it starts so late. I have a bedtime to deal with."

The look of hope turned to confusion, but he didn't ask more. Instead, he said, "Let me upgrade your tickets, you can sit right behind me. I haven't seen anyone in those seats yet, so I'm sure I can get them for you."

"I really appreciate your offer, but my seats are perfect for me, and they actually are behind you, just a bit farther up in the section." He didn't press, and we got up so I could take him home. I folded the blankets and he put them over his arm and grabbed my hand for the walk back. The one thing he never asked about was how I had a key to a fenced-off beach. That was good because that is something I wasn't going to talk about.

The short walk back to my truck was quiet. I went to the driver's side and opened the back door. I took the blankets from his arms and threw them on the seat. I turned back to find myself once again encapsulated by him. He didn't say anything, instead he just stood there and smiled. After what seemed like forever, his hand reached up to my neck, and his thumb stroked my jawline. In the same motion he lowered his mouth to mine and our lips touched. Eyes closed, I savored the contact. First very chaste, then teasing more. My hand raised to his shoulder as his tongue traced over part of my lips. In all my life I had never felt a kiss like this. It was delicate and sexy, possessive and freeing. One of those kisses that makes you weak in the knees. I didn't even realize that I was on my toes until I felt him holding me up when we parted. He was holding me close and whispered in my ear, "I am so glad I didn't hear anything about not kissing on the first date because I don't think I could have waited much longer for that. Now that I've had it, I'm going to need it again." But as he said it, he let me go. He opened my door and I got in. I had only a few seconds to catch my breath and set my mind right before he was opening up the passenger door and sliding in next to me. I had a white-knuckle grip on the steering wheel as I backed down the drive. It was another quiet trip as I made my way back toward downtown. Jayson had mentioned that he was in the loft near the stadium, and I couldn't get there fast enough. If I didn't get him out of the car soon, there was going to be a lot more rule breaking.

I pulled up in front of the building at almost 5 AM. The sun was just starting to rise, and the weight of the evening was crashing down on me.

Jayson hopped out, but before he closed the door he said, "Text me when you get home, so I know you made it safe."

Letting out both a smile and a sigh, "I will." And I did.

Chapter 5

Crush Crush Crush

I usually sleep in a little on Sunday, but this was by far the latest I've slept in a very long time. It was after eleven when I finally got around to peeling myself out of bed. I had crashed very hard. It could have been the cathartic release of telling my story to someone, but more than likely it was that kiss. Holy hell, that kiss. Even thinking about it left me breathless. What was it about him? There was that nagging voice in my head that said he kisses like that because all he does is practice on women all over the country, while the other little voice was saying it was all because of some magical connection. I wanted to believe in magic, but the other reason was so much more likely. If he kissed all those women the way he kissed me last night, it's a miracle he is able to walk outside without being hounded by them all. In the middle of my mental chaos, I heard the ping of my phone.

Jayson: I would really like for you to take my offer of the closer seats. I need to see you tonight.
Cadie: I told you, my seats are perfect for me. I do appreciate your offer, though.

Jayson: If you won't sit in the seats, come down to the
fence during warm-ups. I need to see you.

That was the second time he said that. "I need to see you."
Why? I am still floored that he wanted to see me in the first
place. He is just not the kind of guy I normally see. Don't get
me wrong, he is the most beautiful man I have ever laid eyes
on. He has also been very kind and chivalrous. That's what
doesn't make sense. How could he be interested in me when
there are all those model types throwing themselves at him?

Cadie: I'm sorry. I'm sure there are plenty of beautiful
young women who would kill for those seats. Why not
share with one of them?

Jayson: I offered them to a beautiful, young woman. I
just can't seem to get her to agree to accept them.

Cadie: I've seen the pictures, Jayson. I'm not even close
to the women you are seen with.

Jayson: I know, you are far better than any of them. And
you only see the pictures, you need to actually look at
them. Please don't count me out because of what you
think you see. I'm not that guy at all. Look closer. If I
can't see you at the game, can I at least call you? I need
to see you, but I will settle for hearing from you. Think
about it.

What? This isn't happening, right? I am twenty-six, and no
guy has ever said those kinds of things. Is his game really this
good? Let's be honest, it's working. But it is leading me right
down the path of heartbreak. Strangely, it appears as though
I'm running down the path willingly.

Cadie: We can talk tonight. Have a good game.

I didn't hear back, and I wasn't sure if that was a good thing
or not. Did I piss him off with my refusal, or did he actually
accept my choice and moved on? It didn't seem to matter
what the reason was, I couldn't stop thinking about him. That
smile, those lips, his big, calloused hands. All of it left me in
a clouded haze for the rest of the day.

I took most of the day to clean my house and play outside with Einstein. He is a beast of a dog, and exactly what a single gal who lived on her own needed. He is playful despite his massive frame. On more than one occasion, he knocked me down after running at me a little too fast to return a thrown ball. His loud bark keeps strangers at bay, but those who were invited guests were treated to the presence of a one-hundred-forty-pound lap dog. I love that dog and he keeps me safe. He tired himself out fairly quickly, and was ready to go in for a nap just as I was ready to get showered and changed for the evening. Einstein took his spot on the couch, and I went upstairs to get dressed.

***

It was about six when I pulled up to Cindy's place. She was one of the few people I had gone to high school with whom I was still in contact with. We didn't really know each other then since she was two years younger than me, but we were reacquainted a couple years ago while I was working with the local parks and recreation department summer t-ball program. That summer I helped her son play ball for the first time. Kenneth is eight now and he has cerebral palsy. He has been in a wheelchair most of his life, but it doesn't seem to slow him down one bit. He loves sports and wants to play them all. I try to help as much as I can in that department. Cindy is a single mom and has been since the beginning. I don't know all of the details, but when his condition was diagnosed, his father split. Being that young and then having that responsibility thrust on you couldn't have been easy. The stress made Cindy look well older than her twenty-four years, but she was always upbeat. I respected that.

Cindy greeted me at the door with a huge smile. Apparently, Kenneth has been asking all day if it was time to go. She was going to appreciate this brief time off for more than one reason. I heard Kenneth before I saw him wheel toward the door. He was excited and more than ready to go. I didn't get to step inside. He practically ran his mom over trying to get out of the door. This motorized chair was a blessing and a curse! It really helped him to be more independent, but it also helped him be independent. He zipped out the door, and all we could do was follow. Kenneth was pulled up right next to the back door of my Escalade and was doing whatever he could to help remove his seat belts. While Cindy would have preferred that we took her van and kept him in his chair, she trusted that I would keep him safe, and allowed me to drive my car.

I opened the door and then finished unbuckling his belts. I leaned forward to get his arms around my neck, and then with a little bend of my knees I scooped my arms under his legs and lifted him up into the waiting car seat. He wasn't too heavy, and was still able to sit in a toddler chair even though he was eight. It was perfect because it was safe, and it supported him the way he needed. As I was getting the buckles all done up, Cindy was reminding me about watching what he ate, sticking to soft food and liquids, not letting him get too hot or too cold, all of the mom things she was supposed to say. With a conspiratory wink I looked at Kenneth and said, "I guess that means we have to stick to slushies, cotton candy, and those baseball helmet sundaes."

"What team?" he asked in his disjointed voice.

I replied, "Tonight, I think they are doing something special. I don't think you will have this one."

Cindy just rolled her eyes and then leaned in to kiss her boy. She also gave him the rundown on manners and listening to me while we were out. One more reminder to me about not being out too late, and we were on our way. I sure hope she relaxes for a few hours.

We made it to the stadium well ahead of the 7:05 first pitch, but it always took me a little longer to get us in and situated when I was on my own. Luckily, we were in our seats just ahead of the announcement of the starting line-ups. Each player took the field with a tip of their hat as their name was called. The last guy out was greeted with thunderous applause. Jayson stepped on the field, and I swear he was scanning my section. I probably cheered a little louder than I should. Kenneth was excited, too, and that made me even happier.

I spent the game talking to my little buddy, making sure he had everything his heart desired from the foam bear paw, to the mini bat, to the giant sundae in the helmet. He only took a few bites of it, but it was so worth it seeing the joy on his face. I also kept a very close eye on number 34. He would look up in the stands, but we never connected. I was fine with it, I think. No, I wasn't. I wanted him to see me.

It was getting late, and Kenneth was getting tired, so I decided it was time to call it a night, even though the game wasn't over yet. I was at the top of the aisle, ready to push Kenneth toward the exit, when I heard, "Coach Collins!" I looked around, and then down at the field. He was standing right next to the net with his facemask and helmet tucked under his arm smiling and giving me a wave. Heat overtook my face and I quickly waved back. I saw a very satisfied smile creep toward his eyes as he ducked down and into the dugout.

Kenneth gabbed the whole way home, and I just smiled and listened. But a few minutes before we pulled up to his house it got very quiet, he was sound asleep. Cindy was waiting at the window when we arrived, I hoped she hadn't been waiting too long. She scooped her boy up and I followed her in with all of his treasures. I didn't stay any longer than it took me to drop the stuff in the kitchen because I knew getting him ready for bed was a process. She thanked me once again, unnecessarily, and I was headed home. Before I backed out of the drive, I sent a quick message:

Cadie: Call me when you get home so that I know you are safe.

Yeah, I had borrowed his line, but it was appropriate, and I wanted to let him know that he could still call if he wanted to. I sure hope he wanted to. Seeing him tonight in his element, and then our brief and distant greeting, lit something inside me that I hadn't felt before. Except I had. I felt it when he kissed me. A smile covered my face as I drove home, eagerly waiting for my phone to ring.

Chapter 6

The Kill

My heart skipped a beat when my phone rang out. I was sitting on the couch with Einstein mostly in my lap. He was fast asleep, and he jumped too. The large dog jumping off my lap caused me to answer the phone with a strangled, "Hello?"

"Cadie? Are you okay?" Jayson had concern in his voice.

"Yeah, sorry. The ringer was loud, and it caused my puppy to jump off my lap. He just startled me is all." It was only a half explanation. Was I supposed to say that I had been sitting on my couch, clutching my phone, willing him to call?

The conversation was easy with Jayson. He asked about my day and about the game. I wasn't overly forthcoming, even though I felt like I could share my deepest secrets. This shouldn't be as comfortable as it was. Jayson spoke about the game and how he was feeling better every day after the injury. That's when reality struck me. He doesn't live here. He lived almost three-thousand miles away in North Carolina. This was all temporary, and he was going to be gone sooner rather than later. Normally this was an ideal situation. I could roll around with a super-hot god, and then he would be gone. Except Jayson was different, and I wanted more.

"So, what do you think?" he asked.

"Um, what?" I was obviously lost in my own thoughts and had missed most of what he said.

"I said we should get breakfast in the morning. The weekend is just about over, so you aren't breaking any rules saying yes. We have a day game, but I'm not playing, so I can eat a little heavier than I usually would."

My stupid mouth shot him down before my brain could come up with a better solution. "We already have plans for dinner, and I have a training run in the morning; it probably won't leave enough time for you to eat after and be ready for the game." I guess that really wasn't me shooting him down. I did have a run, and he probably had to be at the park pretty early since the game was at noon. Maybe my brain did have control this time.

"How early and where are you running? Can I come with you?" Jayson was asking and not just inviting himself. I like that, so I went ahead and told him, "It will be really early. Five thirty at the big park on the northside of town. You are welcome to join me, but I don't think I can manage to get myself up much earlier to pick you up. Are you able to meet me there?"

I think I could hear the mischievous smile through the phone, "Nothing would make me happier than waking up in a few hours to spend time with you all sweaty." He was being sexy and sweet, and most importantly sincere. Those things don't often go together. I just laughed and told him I would drop a pin where he should meet me, and reminded him not to be late. A brief yawn escaped, and he said, "Goodnight, Coach Collins. I'll see you in the morning." And then the line was dead.

I tossed and turned for the rest of the night. I thought about what I was going to wear and if I was going to make an ass of myself trying to exercise with a professional athlete. Of course, I was. While I had once been incredibly fit, that wasn't a priority for me anymore. I very much enjoyed food, and the exercise I got was usually with the P.E. teacher and my students. The one constant for me was running. I made sure to do it at least four times a week, even though it wasn't ideal for my back. I signed up for one of those fun, community 5k races every month. This last month I had really stepped it up because I had committed to running a half-marathon in November with Kenneth. Something like that was way out of my comfort and fitness zone, so I had to be diligent in maintaining my training schedule especially since I would be pushing a wheelchair during the race. Monday morning's run was only about five miles, but there were hills, and that was something that I wasn't used to yet.

I stayed in bed until the last possible moment. Since I had already thought too much about what I was going to wear the night before, I would be able to just grab clothes and go. It wasn't until I peeled myself from bed that I wanted a shower. A quick wash and refresh before I spent a bit too much time on my hair. Pulling on a very cute pair of capris and a tech tee, I was out the door. As I drove, I remembered to drop a pin so Jayson knew where to meet me. He would be able to be dropped on the street and find me easy. The closer I got to the park, the more my stomach tangled in knots. Why was he affecting me the way that he was? I never felt like this about the guys I met or those I chose to spend time with. Keep them at arm's length was always the safe bet. Now wasn't a good time to go all in.

My leg was propped up on the cement planter, and I was bent forward in a stretch when an arm snaked around my waist and pulled me up. Back to front, with my head not quite reaching his shoulder, he pressed his mouth to my ear, and in a low growl said, "Running with a raging hard-on is going to be very difficult." I couldn't help but laugh as he pulled me tighter. Immediately I knew that he wasn't kidding. Pressed right up to my lower back was something that until now I thought only existed in the naughty books I tended to read. As with everything else about him, this was a surprise. Big, hard, and nearly touching me. The only separation was a few thin layers of clothes and the crowd of people in the park. It had been my intention to let out an exasperated sigh, but it came out much more like the stupid moan I made when he first helped me into the car. I couldn't face him yet because I knew my eyes would immediately look right at it. Let's be honest, I wanted to look, but I also knew that doing so would end badly. Instead, I turned on my heel to break away. He let me go, and just as I made my first step toward the trail, a large palm hit my ass resulting in a loud smack. I jumped and laughed at the same time. For all intents and purposes, this should be very uncomfortable, but it wasn't. It felt like we had known each other forever, when we really didn't know one another at all. I tapped on my watch and started down the path in a very slow jog. My resolve lasted about thirty seconds before I had to steal that first look. Holy hell, I was in trouble. Jayson was a god. He was wearing his team's athletic shorts, and a short-sleeve shirt. Thick, black hair was pushed back away from his face with one of those elastic headbands that girls usually wore to keep their fine hair out of their faces. On him, there was nothing feminine about it. Sexy. That's the only word that could describe how it looked seeing his face free of cover from his hair or a hat. Deep brown eyes stared back at me and burned into my already-hot skin. And then that smile. When he looked at me it met his eyes. It was both friendly and dangerous. Like an animal that was innocent enough to let you get close enough to pounce on you. That's what it was, Jayson was like a predator. He loomed over me in a provocative way just waiting to jump. Damn, every cell in my body hoped he jumped soon!

As we jogged through the park, I talked about training for the race that was happening much sooner than I had been prepared for. I had let him know that my watch was going to be telling me to pick up the pace soon, and while I was already a sweaty mess, he was barely getting warmed up. This is exactly what I knew was going to happen. I was going to look like a wet rag, and he was going to be a god with a delicious glow. He already did.

Just like the night before on the phone conversation was easy. We talked more about him and baseball, and he asked about my family and work. While they were getting-to-know-you type of questions, answering them felt safe and easy. My guard was dropping, and I didn't even really notice. After about an hour, we had made it back to where we started. We had stopped to catch our breath for a minute, or I did because Jayson wasn't even winded, when he turned to face me. Gently, he brushed a few stray strands of hair back behind my ear. It was a very tender gesture, but his touch sent a bolt of electricity straight to my core. Jayson was looking at my eyes as if he were contemplating something. He reached out for me and he leaned down and placed a very chaste kiss first on my lips and then my forehead. His chin rested on the top of my head and I took a deep breath in. Spice, sweat, it was all man. He smelled like something so appealing that I wanted it to envelop me, it did. His arms were around me, pulling me tight. There was a big sigh. I knew he was thinking the same thing I was about this situation being temporary. In a few days or a few weeks, he could be gone. He could be gone away from me before this even started. I didn't want to think about it, and it was obvious that neither did he. I grabbed him by the hand and pulled him across the street to the coffee shop.

I told him to get us a table and asked what he wanted. I made my way to the line and placed our order. Luckily it was still early, so everything was made quickly, and he had just taken a seat when I approached with our food and coffee. He was sitting with his back to the door facing away from most of the people. I know now he did it so he could avoid being bothered by people. The hard thing is, he stood out. Jayson was a large man, and just gave off a certain confident vibe. He was also ridiculously good looking. Even if he hadn't been a professional baseball player, he would attract attention. Settling into the table, I took a long drink from my coffee, closed my eyes, and relaxed a fraction. Jayson, however, dug right into his food. It is very possible that he took maybe four or five bites before he was done. With a little laugh, I gestured toward mine, and without hesitation he devoured that one too. I couldn't help but sit there and smile. When he was eating, he looked so carefree, which was very different from the confident professional look he typically wore.

We sat and enjoyed our coffee for a while before the interruptions started. At first it was just one person being overly polite and embarrassed for bothering us, but as soon as that person was gone, the next was upon him. After almost thirty minutes of constant interruptions, and during one brief break, he said, "This is fucking retarded! I can't even have a simple coffee date without being interrupted for some bullshit." He wasn't keeping his voice down and I was able to see a few people back away. I was glad they did because now was the time for the talk.

"Don't use that word, please," was all I was able to get out at first. He looked at me, trying to pick the offending word. Not being able to choose between the swear words he'd said, he sat quietly. "The word 'retard'. Pick another adverb." I was being very clipped with my words because I wanted to be calm. "When you use that word, I assume you mean stupid or upsetting, right? But when you hear that word, what do you picture in your mind?" I asked. "Go ahead, tell me what you see in your mind when you hear the word 'retard'." I was prodding him.

Finally, he described to me exactly what I knew he would. The broken body, a twisted hand or arm, a slack face. In my most collected voice, I said, "You understand that people who look that way and have those types of disabilities didn't choose that life for themselves, right? No parent ever thinks that the child that they are carrying will be considered 'less than' by the community. They didn't sign up for a

44

lifetime of challenges and unsolicited looks. They don't have the ability to tell people off or turn down a photo opportunity. Their greatest gift comes from that curse in that maybe they don't see or understand just how awful we can be to one another. Just how hateful words can be." Partway through my talk, Jayson hung his head. When I was done talking, I put my hand to his chin, lifting it to look at me. He was sufficiently embarrassed, even though that wasn't my intent.

"I didn't look at it that way. I guess I never really thought about it." His words were contrite.

"I know you didn't, and that's why this is a lesson and not an admonishment ending with me leaving you stranded," I said in a joking tone to lighten the mood. "It's one of those things you grow up saying, and it isn't until you get older that you realize that your words have power and that you need to choose them carefully. Now you know, and unless you say it again, it isn't an issue in my eyes."

Saying that to him didn't seem to change his mood. Well, at least I was able to instill some wisdom before I scared him off of me for good.

Knowing this was probably the end of the conversation, and more importantly, our time together, I stood up to leave. Jayson grabbed my wrist and asked me to sit back down. Relief flushed over me because I truly didn't want it to end like this. His eyes met mine and he started talking. "I'm sorry. I really am. Thank you. Thank you for taking the time to explain to me why you don't like that word and why people shouldn't use it. More importantly, thank you for caring enough to explain it to me. Not very many people even bother to talk with me about things anymore. I'm told what to do and where to be. I'm given the *Reader's Digest* version of everything in my life because people think I can't be bothered with the details, or worse, that I'm too dumb to understand. While there is no way that I can know what people with disabilities like that are going through, I can sympathize with the feeling of not being enough."

Wait, what? I sat there in complete shock of what Jayson was saying to me. How do I reply to that? What should I say? All I could come up with was, "Feeling not enough is never okay, especially when you are." Not much else could be packed into this conversation, so this time he got up to go, and as he did, he grabbed me by the hand. What happened next was even more of a surprise. Right there in the middle of the coffee shop, he kissed me. Just like he had before. It was passionate and caring and it was very public. I could feel eyes on us, and I could also feel the flush take over me. I was getting all sweaty again, and this time it had nothing to do with physical exertion. Jayson pulled away, once again leaving me breathless.

As we walked toward my car, he asked if I was going to the game today. To be honest, I didn't typically go to the day games. One, I was usually working, and two, it was insanely hot in the middle of the day here in the Valley. I really only wanted to be in my pool or in the air conditioning. "I don't have anyone who will tag along. Cecily hates the heat and will be beating down my door pretty soon to get in my pool," I answered.

With a shrug of his shoulders, he said very casually, "I'm sure you can find someone, if not, you could come alone. I could get you good seats." There was a tone of hopefulness in his voice. We reached my SUV and Jayson had already opened my door and ushered me inside when I decided I couldn't drive home in a sweaty shirt. I hopped back out and opened the door just behind me. In a flash, I had the wet one off and a fresh shirt over my head. Jayson really only had time to whip his head around as I slung the offending shirt on the floorboard. His eyes caught mine, and then they drifted over to the car seat that was still fastened in behind him. He wanted to ask, to say something, but he didn't. At least not until we were right in front of his building.

As he got out, he said, "Why don't you bring your son. Today is one of those games where they let the kids run the bases and then in the sprinklers after."

Even though I knew it was the wrong reaction, I just shook my head and laughed. I should have just told him I didn't have children. There was that ornery part of me that liked to watch him twist just a bit. Finally, I said with a shrug, "We'll see."

As soon as he ducked into the building, I decided to make some calls. Jayson wanted me at that game in just a few hours, and I was going to be there. Calling Cindy first was going to be my best bet. She picked up right away, and lucky for me she agreed, even though we had just been the night before. I asked if she wanted to come along this time, but she declined. I know these little breaks are important to her, even if she won't admit it. The game was scheduled to start at twelve thirty, but since I didn't want to sit in the hot sun for hours, I let Cindy know I'd pick Kenneth up closer to one thirty. We could enjoy a few innings and then we could have a little fun on the field. My next call was to my bother-in-law to see if he could help with getting me down on the field after the game. It wasn't like we could just hop over the short fence, we would need a ramp and probably some space.

**

Thankfully, the game was over not long after we had arrived. The players wanted to be done with this heat as much as the small crowd in the stands. Today's group was mostly families that were there to enjoy the stadium and all of the fun things they were doing for the kids. One of the advantages of needing wheelchair access was we didn't have to wait in the crush of people ready to push through the two small gates that led onto the field. I walked Kenneth down the concourse to a ramp near right field. This is usually where the mascot enters on his quad. Phillip met me there and gave Kenneth a fist bump, asking him if he was ready to run the bases and get wet in the sprinklers. He had an ear-to-ear grin, and was getting more excited with each step I took and was only able to manage a squeaky, "Yes!" Phil just laughed and then looked at me and asked if I was ready for the same. "You know how much I love these kids. I would do anything to make sure they get to have these experiences."

He shook his head at me and said, "You are a saint."

It was my turn to laugh, "Well, I have a lot of repenting to do." We were on the field, and by now most of the kids had abandoned the bases for the outfield of sprinklers. Phil asked if I needed any help, and I waved him off. "I got this. I know you have other stuff to deal with. We really appreciate you helping us today." He gave Kenneth one more fist bump and then disappeared into the dugout.

I took Kenneth out of the jogging stroller and had him propped up against my side as I straightened out his legs. He wasn't going to be running those bases, but I was going to have him take a few steps. I held tight around his waist as his little feet tried as best as they could to make a running motion. This wasn't exactly an ideal situation to run in, being bent forward with close to fifty pounds of unsupported weight out front, but I had his feet just high enough off the ground that neither of us would get tripped up, and then I took off. Kenneth squealed with laughter as we rounded each base. When we touched third, I made eye contact with him. Knowing I couldn't slow down and ruin the fun, I kept on going strong until we hit home. Ready to sit down because I was winded, Kenneth shouted, "More!" There was no way I could tell him no, so I said, "Okay, but this time you have to ride in the back." He didn't protest, and somehow I managed to get him on my back without having to set him all the way back down. Again, this wasn't an easy way to run since he didn't really have the ability to hold on tight, but I could manage him much easier on my back. Two more trips around and I was done. My back was screaming, and I couldn't do another lap. Luckily, Kenneth didn't protest when I sat us down. We were both sitting on the grass when Jayson finally came over.

He crouched down next to us and extended his hand to Kenneth to introduce himself. Kenneth tried his best to reach back, and Jayson took his hand and said, "My name's Jayson. What's yours?" There were all kinds of excited sounds coming from Kenneth, and none of them were his name. I could tell he was so excited to meet one of the guys wearing a uniform, that getting his name out was going to be a problem.

"Jayson, this is Kenneth," I interjected. If there was a time to have cameras rolling, it was now.

The look on Jayson's face was pure confusion. Again, speaking to Kenneth, he asked, "Do you come to the games with your mom often?" This time Kenneth was able to get out a few words in his laughter, "Not. Mom. Coach." I was laughing hysterically as Jayson's confusion grew. It was time to let him off the hook. "If it wasn't entirely obvious, Kenneth isn't my son. I coach his t-ball team." It wasn't so much a sense of relief that I saw in Jayson, but more of a look of understanding. What the obvious part of the whole equation was that Kenneth was black. Well, half black and half Hispanic. It would be nearly impossible for a kid with mocha skin and black hair to have come from me. I could sense that Kenneth didn't quite understand why I was laughing so hard, so I said, "Kenneth, my friend Jayson thought that I was your mommy." He immediately started laughing too. With an exasperated look, Jayson finally sat all the way down.

Right before his gorgeous ass hit the grass, he had reached in his back pocket and pulled out a ball. Holding it up, he asked Kenneth if he wanted to play catch. Kenneth nodded enthusiastically and put his hands up to catch a thrown ball. Quickly, I interjected, "Maybe we should start with some grounders." Moving myself to Kenneth's side, I arranged his legs in a V sitting opposite of Jayson. He mirrored the position, stretching his long legs out on either side of Kenneth's.

As they rolled the ball back and forth with little interference from me, Jayson asked, "How long were you going to let me swing?"

Amused, I answered, "You were the one who made the assumptions instead of just asking. To be honest, I was really impressed that you were still interested even when you thought I was a single mom. I know you saw the jogger in my trunk Saturday night, and you wanted to ask then. But you didn't, and instead you just wanted to get to know me. That means a lot."

"I think I told you on more than one occasion that I am not the guy everyone thinks I am. I like you, and if that was part of you, then I would accept that." Damn, there he goes again with that honesty and sincerity. He isn't the guy everyone says he is. Now, I really need to find out just who that is.

Both Kenneth and I needed to get out of the sun, so I said, "It's time we say goodbye so I can get you home before naptime."

Quickly and surprisingly clear, Kenneth blurted, "No nap!" He obviously didn't want to look like a "little kid" in front of Jayson.

Playing right along, Jayson looked down at his watch and said, "You are right, it is almost naptime. If I don't take mine, I will be super grouchy later."

All Kenneth said was, "Nap!" In yet another surprising move, Jayson scooped Kenneth up and got him seated in the jogger. After getting the buckles done up, I thanked Jayson for his time and patience. He moved his hand to the small of my back before quickly pulling it back when I winced. "Are we still on for dinner?" he asked me quietly. I nodded and let him know I would send him a text when I got home. He gave Kenneth one more fist bump and made sure the ball was tight in his grasp before we walked our separate ways.

Chapter 7

Dance With Me Tonight

As soon as I got home, I sent Jayson a message asking him about dinner. On my way through the house, I gave Einstein a rub and picked up my MacBook from the office. There was still plenty of time for me to do a little internet "research" and take Einstein out for a walk before I needed to get ready for my date. Flopping myself down on the bed, I opened my laptop and typed his name into the browser. There were the obvious baseball-related stories, as well as a Wiki page about him that I grazed quickly for some facts. It was all very general. He was thirty years old, from North Carolina, six two, baseball stuff, college stuff, and then a whole section on his personal life. I knew better than to believe all the crap that people post on the Internet, but it was interesting, nonetheless. It mentioned a long-time girlfriend, and then after their split he was never seen with the same woman twice. The bit of information about the former girlfriend part piqued my interest. We all have exes, except me. Technically, I never really had a boyfriend. I've dated, but had never made anything serious. All of my gentleman friends were kept at arm's length when it came to the feelings stuff. From the article, as well as the numerous non-baseball pictures, it also seems like Jayson keeps women, at least in terms of serious relationships, at a distance. Every single woman he was with is model gorgeous. Actually, I think most of them are models and actresses. That is so not me. The thought of even being in a picture like that with Jayson turns my stomach. I've already had people gossip about my personal life, and that was before the Internet. I can't imagine what people would write about me if they saw me with Jayson. Forget small-town rumors. I'm no model, and they will tear me to pieces. Getting out of this now will spare me the soul crushing that is bound to happen. But it wouldn't be fair to either of us to not try because I was carrying scars from my past.

Turning back to the internet search, I learned a lot more. There were lots of baseball pictures, some even going back to when he played in college. But a majority of the pictures I saw were fan pictures. All of those "fans" happened to be women. Each and every picture included a woman or two draped all over him. His smile was the same in each picture. It was pleasant, but not honest. He made sure he looked happy; it just wasn't genuine. It never touched his eyes. I also noticed something else that was even more interesting than his smile, his arms. In each and every photo, his arms were crossed on his chest, held out wide with hands in a peace sign or horns, or flexed like a bodybuilder. His hands were never touching anyone in the picture. Every picture was the same, hands visible and not making contact with anyone other than himself. Maybe he wasn't the womanizer everyone thought he was? Sure, the more formal pictures were with dates, but when I looked closer, I saw that same smile. Pleasant and friendly, but not authentic. He would have a hand at their back, but never too low, and none holding hands with these women. They were there for the show.

It wasn't until my phone rang that I realized I had been staring at my computer for an hour. Jayson was calling. Shit,

I had been so engrossed in what I was doing that I didn't respond to any of his texts. In my typical fashion, I skipped the greeting and started with an apology. "Jayson, I am so sorry I didn't respond. I was doing some work on my computer and lost track of time."

"It's good to hear you weren't just ignoring me. You had me worried that you were going to bail on me." I actually could hear the relief in his voice. "No, sometimes I just fall down a rabbit hole on the computer. Any ideas on what kind of food you want for dinner? I don't figure you have any particular place in mind?" I asked.

"I am going to leave this one up to you. I am not picky when it comes to food. My only request is that there is a chance that we can eat with few interruptions?"

"If you don't mind something pretty laid back, one of my good friends owns a Mexican restaurant here in town, and he will take care of us. Are you fine with something a little out of the way? The food is amazing, and I know we can eat in peace."

Before I was able to get out any other details, he said, "That sounds incredible! Are you sure it's not a big deal to impose on your friend?"

"Of course not. Will seven work? Taking a car out here isn't worth the expense, so I can come and get you if you like?" There was laughing on the other end of the line.

"You must really not want me to know where you live if you don't want me to take a car out there. The cost is not exactly prohibitive for me. But if it allows me to spend even longer with you in a car, I won't turn you down. I'll meet you out front at seven." And then he hung up. It hadn't really crossed my mind that he had money. That was never important to me. Just because he had it, didn't mean he should spend it.

Looking at the clock, I realized I had a lot less time to get ready than I had originally thought. I ran downstairs to set the ball toy up for Einstein in the backyard. He wasn't going to get a walk today, not that he minded. He was content in the yard, so I went about readying myself. I smoothed lotion on every square inch of me, making sure there wasn't any ashy bits. It was my hair I was worried about. Day to day I didn't fuss that much with it. On its own, it was a bit wild. If I didn't take hot tools to it, I was a lot more Merida than Ariel. I figured if I was actually going on a real date, I would do real date hair. I took my time to blow it out with a flat brush before I set it in rollers. While my hair set, I applied my makeup. I loved sitting at my vanity and putting on a full face. It didn't happen very often because it would melt off teaching and coaching. But on the weekends and special occasions, I did it up. Cat eyes and red lips were my signature.

From my closet I picked out a cute summer dress that was black with pink polka dots. The dress was vintage, and I paired it with a cute black shrug and some black and pink heels. It was pin-up casual. My excitement for the evening had me reaching for the "good underwear" drawer, selecting a matching bra and panty. I only care if they match if there is a possibility of someone else seeing me in them, and tonight, I hope someone would.

I had my hair brushed out in a soft wave down my back in just a few minutes. As I was smoothing out the last bit, I realized I never called Matt or Natalia at the restaurant. Luckily, Natalia picked up right away and said that it wouldn't be a problem. Mondays weren't typically busy, but she and Matt would make sure we weren't bothered. I added some cute earrings and ditched my smartwatch. I covered my tan line with a bracelet, and I was out the door.

I hate being late, even if it is a couple minutes. Knowing that, I sent Jayson a quick text that I was running behind by a couple minutes, but I'd be there in a few. When I pulled up at the curb, it was 7:03. He was standing there holding a bouquet of flowers and looking deliciously fresh from the shower. His effort was noted but not obvious. Simple jeans and a black V-neck shirt, his hair still damp from the shower, but pulled back in a small knot. He was trying to kill me with that smile, or at least set fire to my panties. I put the car in park when I saw him step around to the driver's side. He opened the door and took my hand. I slid down off the high seat in my SUV and he took me in his arms. I was greeted by an embrace and a kiss, along with flowers and far too many compliments. Not even giving it a second thought, I slipped the keys in his hand as he walked me toward the passenger side. Once I was safely buckled in, he moved gracefully back to the driver's side, adjusting the seat pretty far back before he even attempted to get in. He had to make a few more adjustments before he was ready to go. I just sat in awe of him. Jayson was so incredibly handsome, and you could see the flex of every muscle as he moved. Each move was deliberate, not wasteful. It was like watching a beautiful big cat stalk the jungle. I was abruptly snatched from my fantasy when I heard him ask for probably the second time just where we were going. Oh yeah, he was driving in an unfamiliar town to an unknown restaurant in a neighboring town. I tapped on the screen on the dash and said, "Jamie, bring up turn by turn directions to Vela's." My digital assistant immediately started giving directions, and Jayson followed. It was an easy drive, and I am sure I spent most of it just staring at just how incredibly gorgeous the guy driving me was. My mind wandered as I thought about kissing him along his sharp jaw, and just about anywhere else on his incredible body. This was going to be a long drive and a very long dinner.

When he had turned on to the main street that Vela's was located on, I motioned for him to pull into the alleyway so that we could park off the street. It was really quiet out back, which was a sign that inside would be quiet too.

Matt greeted us as soon as Jayson opened the door. It took just a second for him to place my date, but he didn't make mention of it. I waited until we were seated to introduce them, and Matt was gracious enough not to make a big deal out of him. He wasn't so gracious when it came to me and said, "It's about time you had a date, Cadie. I was getting ready to have Natalia go to your house to make sure you hadn't started on a cat collection." I laughed along with him, only to keep myself from choking him out in his own restaurant. Jayson looked amused, but smartly declined to comment.

Matt hadn't brought over any menus since I usually just ate whatever they brought. I loved just about everything here, and his cousin who was the cook knew what I wasn't a fan of. He did ask if I wanted my usual drink, and then asked Jayson what he might want. He was polite and just said that he would have whatever I was having. Matt excused himself, letting us know that his wife would bring our drinks over, as well as some chips and salsa. The confused look on Jayson's face finally registered with me, so I said, "I come here all the time and I eat whatever they bring out. I will ask Natalia for a menu unless you know what kinds of things you like. You can pretty much ask for whatever and they will make it." I found myself apologizing as I was talking, "I'm so sorry, I didn't even think that this isn't what you are accustomed to."

Jayson put his hand on mine and said, "Relax, this is actually quite refreshing. I told you I wasn't picky, and I think it is amazing that places like this exist. It's the kind of shit you see in the movies or on TV. They know you and they feed you like a member of their own family. I like it."

The tension released from my shoulders just as Natalia set two very large red beers on the table with some chips and salsa. "Before I come back with a couple waters, you must introduce me to your very handsome date, Cadie. I was getting ready to go search your place for your cat collection."

This time Jayson let out a laugh as he extended his hand. "Natalia, this is my friend Jayson. Jayson, this is my former friend Natalia." They both laughed and I twisted in my seat. Natalia let me stew for just a few seconds before she said, "I know exactly who this is, and if he knows what's good for him, he will remember that you have good friends who look out for you and also happen to be fixing his dinner." That's what I loved about my small circle of friends. They would roast me right to my face, but wouldn't bat an eye about burying a body. She dropped off the waters at the table and was gone without taking our order. We were just going to get food and be left alone.

We ate and conversed for over an hour. Things were light, but there was something that wasn't being said. While I'm sure it had to do with whatever was going on between us, I wasn't about to open up that can of worms. Cadie didn't date. Not until tonight. Cadie didn't have feelings for the opposite sex. Not until this man made me blush with just a few words. Things like this just don't happen to me. He has been nothing but kind, thoughtful, and incredibly sexy. The longer I looked across the table at him, the more I wanted to jump over it and devour him.

Caught in my daydream again, he said, "Did you hear what I said?"

I hadn't, I was too busy just looking at his mouth as it moved, wanting it to be on me. "I'm headed back to Raleigh on Wednesday. The doctor says I can return to the team."

Closing my eyes and taking a breath to make sure I wasn't just lost in thought again, I let those words sink in. He was leaving. Whatever this was hadn't even started. It had only been a few days, but I had let him pass gates that no man had even come close to seeing. I liked him and I barely knew him. This hurt way more than it should. Jayson put his hand over mine and spoke very softly. "I know this is absolutely crazy, but I don't want this to be over before we even get the chance to see if it could be something. In two days you have made me absolutely crazy. I can't get you out of my mind, and I don't want to. I want more with you, Cadie. I need the next thirty-six hours to show you that you can trust what I say. I need you to give this a chance."

Was I hearing this right? An incredibly handsome, baseball god wanted to try and date me when he lived some three-thousand miles away. What can a person even say to that? Before my brain had a chance to catch up to my mouth, I said, "Okay." His grip tightened on my hand and he smiled that wicked smile that went straight to my core. I pressed my thighs together under the table for any sort of relief. The decision to take Jayson to bed had been made way earlier that evening, but the decision to break my rules happened when he looked at me that way.

I stood up and dropped some money on the table. At this point I was basically dragging him back to my car. I gave him clipped directions to my house. If we didn't just get there, I was sure I would lose my nerve. When we turned the corner, I instructed him to pull into the drive and just off to the left of the garage. A few taps on my phone and the garage door started to open. I let him open my door so I could have a quick moment to catch my breath. He held his hand out for me as I stepped down, and immediately he pulled me in for a kiss. Jayson was claiming me with this kiss. His tongue had parted my lips and was exploring and wanting more. He pulled away and I was breathless.

We both turned toward the house, then he stopped short to look at the two cars in the garage. One was shiny, black, small, and sporty. The other was big and a flat black, same as my Escalade. Jayson looked at me with curious confusion. I shrugged a shoulder and said, "One is fun, and one is fast. I actually drive that one," pointing to my CT5-V, "on a daily basis. It's only when I'm taking gear or people that I drive the Escalade." I hadn't said anything about the classic Chevelle, so he did.

"And when do you drive that one?"

"On the rarest of occasion, because I still have problems with it that I just can't figure out. I don't really have the time. But it was my grandpa's and I will never part with it."

Jayson snaked his arm around my waist and said, "I know what you mean."

He followed me into the house through the garage, but froze in his tracks when Einstein rounded the corner into the kitchen. Before he made it past me, I snapped my fingers and told him to sit. He immediately sat at my feet. "Umm, is that your puppy?" he asked, pointing at the beast at my side.

"Yep! He really is still a puppy since he's just over a year old. I kind of forget how big he actually is. Sorry," I said apologetically. "Just hold your hand out so he can smell it. Since you walked in with me, he won't eat you unless I tell him to." I was only half joking. Einstein was crazy protective, but people who came to my house quickly learned that he was a pushover. Jayson walked over and Einstein smelled his hand but didn't move from his spot. It was his dinner time, and he was going to bug me until he ate. I fed him quickly and extended my hand to Jayson to give him the house tour.

We moved into the next room, leaving Einstein in the kitchen. The house wasn't dark, but we needed more lights. I spoke out loud, and the virtual assistant answered, "Good evening, Cadie. What are your plans for the night?" I laughed and Jayson swallowed hard. "Let's just chill out for the rest of the night, but first we need to do a house tour." I was talking to the house, but also Jayson. There was a click and hiss of speakers coming on, as well as a few more clicks for lights. He was looking around at my house when the very distinct opening to "Welcome to the Jungle" started. It took the tension out of the air, and I could see the amused relief on Jayson. "Just a little joke I programmed in," I said with a smile. A few more chords were played, and the music turned much quieter and softer.

"You said you weren't one of those super geniuses, but your whole life is run by a custom digital assistant. Are you Tony Stark?" I just laughed as I explained that I loved gadgets, and everything in my house was stuff you could buy online. Sure, the programming part took time, but it wasn't complicated. I walked him through the lower level of the house, and we peeked out to the backyard so I could point out the pool and lounge area. I knew where this tour was going to end, so I led him upstairs. With each step, my feet got heavier. The only men to cross the threshold of my bedroom had been the ones who delivered my furniture.

Jayson was on me before I even had the chance to show him all the way in. I wonder if he could tell I was losing my nerve. He was backing me up toward my bed while peeling the sweater from my shoulders. His mouth fused to mine. When my legs hit the bed, he pulled back and caught a glimpse in the mirror. The back of my dress exposed the top of my tattoo that the sweater had covered. Feeling for my side zipper, Jayson leaned into my ear and practically growled, "I have been dreaming of exploring every inch of your skin, and I would have never imagined that it could be made even more beautiful with decoration."

He turned me around and my dress fell to the floor. His hand pressed me forward on the bed, so I was bent at the waist. A single finger traced my spine, followed by sweet kisses. My bra came loose as he moved down my back. The sensual assault continued as he slipped my panties down to my feet. A shiver ran through my whole body, but I was red hot instead of cold.

Jayson turned me once again, lifting me very gently onto my bed. He asked, "Are you okay?" I whispered a yes, already lost in what he was doing to me. His hands never lost contact, and neither did his eyes. His strong hand slid down my leg, and he pulled my ankle up to his mouth. My shoe slipped from my foot as he trailed faint kisses up to my knee. He repeated the process with my left. Keeping one hand on my knee, he reached over his head and pulled his shirt up by the collar, tossing it on the floor. That hand was back on me in a blink, pushing my knees back and apart. He let out a deep breath, "Beautiful." My head was spinning. I wanted him inside of me, but I also wanted to feel him on my skin. His mouth worked up my inner thigh with kisses and small bites. When he reached the apex of my thighs, he took a much deeper bite, sucking the flesh of my inner thigh. His cheek was cool against my hot desire.

I was tied up in knots and needed to feel release. Jayson answered the call with one swipe of his tongue. His lips caressed my most sensitive parts as his tongue ran up my slit and circled my clit. The vibration of the "mmmmmm" that he let out almost sent me over the edge. My hands fisted in his hair, half holding on and half urging him on. Breaths became more like gasps as his tongue flicked over my over sensitive bud. His tongue was dipping ever so slightly inside with each pass. His mouth covered me entirely as he both licked and nibbled on me, drawing out my pleasure. The wave I was riding came crashing down and I called out "Jayson!" as a desperate plea. As my body trembled, he slipped one and then a second finger deep inside me. I was so hyperaware of every move they made as they stroked deep inside. He was building me right back up without letting me down from the first orgasm. His mouth had continued to suck and tease my clit as his fingers stroked in and out. This time I came even harder. I felt myself squeeze down on his fingers deep from within as my thighs hugged his face.

I was finally able to pry my eyes open to see him suck on each of the fingers that had fucked me better than any dick had in my life. He was staring right at me, one hand still on me, as the intruding fingers deftly undid the button and zipper of his jeans. There was nothing that could have prepared me for the enormous erection that sprang from his boxer briefs. What I thought I had figured out from our contact during my run was all wrong. I let out an audible gasp as it brushed his flat stomach. I really didn't have more than a quick glance before he was on me again. He had taken full possession of my body.

He leaned over me and whispered, "You taste better and are juicier than any peach in Georgia." Bites followed kisses, and his tongue soothed every nip that he took down my neck to my chest.

I could feel the calloused skin on his palms and on his fingers as he softly kneaded my breasts. They more than filled his hands, and his mouth claimed every part that spilled over. Pulling and sucking on each of my peaked nipples caused me to arch my back up toward him. I was so lost in his mouth that I let out a surprised scream when he slid inside of me. I was so incredibly full that he had to pause to allow me to adjust to take him all the way.

"Fuck. You are so tight, this isn't going to last long." Last long? My brain was already scrambled, and I couldn't even imagine this going on at all. Long, slow strokes coaxed me back up the hill. I could barely move from all the pleasure that I had already received, but I needed to feel him. My hands ran up his massive arms and found their way to his broad shoulders. I pulled him close so that I could get my mouth on his skin. He tasted like salty, sweet sweat. My nails were sinking into the skin on his back and he encouraged me on, "Come for me, baby. I want to feel you come on my cock."

His words were all I needed to explode. "Oh God. Jayson. Yes!" Once again, I could feel myself squeezing tight, this time urging his release. A few more strokes and I felt him come as he called out, "Cadie!"

He rolled so that I was lying on top of him, not breaking our connection. He was still hard. There was absolutely no way I would be able to survive any more. "Is it your intention to fuck me into submission, or just to death?" He laughed at my question, but I was dead serious. How had I never felt THAT before? I rested there for a minute or two more so I could catch my breath. Just as I started to move, he held on a little tighter.

"Cadie, I didn't wear a condom. I swear I never do that. I never even thought about stopping." Jayson was holding his breath now. Fuck! Careful Cadie would have never let that happen.

"I'm fine," was all the explanation that I could offer. I shouldn't be having this conversation this late in the game. This is supposed to happen way before clothes come off. All of the rules and my senses had completely escaped me.

I was now tucked tightly under Jayson's embrace. My back was to his front as he spoke softly in my ear. "You know there is no way I'm going to give you up now. I've tasted the forbidden fruit, and I am going to come back for seconds and thirds. I will never have enough of you. The way you smell, the way you taste, the way you feel, all of it left me satisfied, but I need more."

With a breathless giggle, I said, "I already had seconds and thirds."

His arms tightened as he said, "We are just getting started." He meant it. We traded orgasms for hours before we both just passed out from exhausted bliss.

A faint ping echoed in the silence as my eyes opened to reveal that this was more than a dream. This was all very real.

Chapter 8

Panic Switch

That familiar ping of an incoming text peeled my eyes open again. A very large, tattooed arm lay across my hips. Lying face down, right next to me, was a mess of inky black curls, broad shoulders, and impossibly large biceps. I started to panic and closed my eyes in a desperate attempt to center myself, then I started to count down. Three, your name is Cadie Collins; two, you are twenty-six years old; and one, you broke all of the rules last night. Carefully, I reached over to grab my phone, trying not to wake the giant. I slid up until my back was pressed up against the oak slats of my sleigh bed, only to feel a grip on my hip as I moved. I quickly unlocked my phone and read the message from my best friend Cecily.

Cecily: Bad gas travels fast in a small town.

I couldn't help but let out a stifled laugh. It happened to be the honest truth. Nothing stayed quiet in this town for long. Ceci must have already heard I had a date from Natalia, and now I need to face the story that is out there. I'm sure it is only my friends keeping me on my toes, but the very real possibility that someone recognized Jayson last night hits me. What if someone took a picture without us knowing? Are people already talking? The hand on my hip flexed again, and when I looked down at him, I was greeted by a beautiful, panty-dropping smile. I looked him over, only to have him bury his face in the pillow and laugh. I squeezed my eyes tight and sigh.

I've already opened the ride share app on my phone and ordered a car, it's only ten minutes away. I'm quiet, I don't know where to start. There are so many things that have happened that never have before. The first being the giant of a man who is lying in my bed with only a soft sheet covering the lower half of his massive frame. His back and shoulders are broad and covered in beautiful art. I never do things like this. Being cautious is something I pride myself on. Carefully, I slid off the bed and pulled a shirt from the floor over my head. I pad down to the bench seat at the foot of my bed and put my head in my hands. The quiet is broken by the sound of my ringing phone. I immediately know who it is. She always calls when I don't immediately answer a text. Like always, I skipped the greeting and got right to it. Quickly, I bark out, "Boxcar in twenty." Without waiting for a reply, I hung up. It's still quiet, but I hear the movement behind me, and then feel the breath on my neck.

"You are going to have to give up my shirt if you are kicking me out." But the thing is, I don't want to. I want nothing more than to climb right back in bed and do it all over again. I've sat still too long. I need to answer, but nothing comes out. "The team won't take rolling around in bed with a beautiful woman all day as an acceptable excuse for me to miss my last morning workout," he says in a husky growl.

"I suppose not, but maybe I could convince you otherwise." I wish I was joking, but I wasn't. This god before me is nothing but heartbreak waiting to happen. The thought isn't even all the way out of my head when I feel his hands reach down and lift the hem of the shirt up and over my head.

But in one quick motion, he pulls it down over himself and kisses the top of my head. As he is walking out of my bedroom door, he says very casually, "I'll see you again tonight, Kitten." And like that, he is gone. I'm sitting naked in my bedroom, head in my hands desperately willing my body to move. Just get up and get dressed, Cadie. Drive to breakfast, talk to Ceci, and figure out just what happens next. Wait, did he just call me Kitten?

Minutes passed, or maybe it was just seconds. Either way, I pulled on some underwear and a dress over my head. My toothbrush hung out of my mouth as I tied my hair up in a top knot. I rushed down the stairs toward the garage and I could feel him before I even saw him. He was sitting on the couch in my living room with Einstein's head in his lap. "I wasn't sure how I was getting back to my apartment, and I didn't want to sit on your front steps like a lost puppy so I decided to wait for you here. This one likes me. I just need to convince you," he said, gesturing toward my dog. Traitor! Why couldn't I get words out? Was my brain really that sex scrambled?

I was just staring at him when, "I need to meet my friend!" finally stumbled out of my mouth. I was gesturing toward the garage, and he grabbed my wrist and pulled me toward him as he stood up.

"Look, Kitten, I know we literally just met, and I'm leaving tomorrow morning, but there is something about you that has me..." he trailed off. "Please come to my apartment after you talk to your friend. I know you want to figure this out, but I need to spend more time with you. We can have dinner and talk. If you don't want to stay, you can just walk away. Just give me a chance to change your mind first."

Jayson was being so sincere, and I didn't get it. All I could say was, "Okay" and then my phone alerted me that the car was outside. He had already pulled me in close and kissed me like he was never going to see me again. The thing is, I knew better. I had already decided I needed more. I just wanted someone to say it was okay. I closed the door behind him and exhaled loudly.

***

Cecily was already seated with coffee and juice for us both when I arrived. She was looking at me very intently, but not saying a word. Yeah, I knew she wasn't going to talk first. My best friend was just going to keep staring at me until I finally just couldn't take it anymore. "I literally broke every single rule last night, Ceci," I said as I slumped down in the chair.

She just giggled and said, "It's about fucking time!" Hold on a minute, she was the one who started me on these rules, and now she was just fine with me throwing them all out the window?

"I don't think you heard me correctly, I literally broke Every. Single. Rule." My last words were punctuated.

"Are you hurt? Did you have a good time? By the looks of it, everything seems to be just fine. I mean, other than the unnecessary look of panic on your face and the sex hair." She was speaking so sensibly, like I was a crazy person for being so wound up.

"Take me through last night. Maybe I can help you figure out why you are being ridiculous." It was just so clear to her, why was I having such a hard time?

"Since you and I are sitting here discussing this, I can assume that you have already heard from Natalia or Matt?" Cecily nodded and waited for me to continue. "Are they the only ones? Do other people know?" I was so nervous about people talking that the fear was overshadowing the real issue. I launched into the story about everything that had happened since I last saw her two nights ago. She just took it in, giving me a reassuring smile as I talked. "Everything was just so easy to talk about. I told him about school and the accident, and he knows about my job, and it was all just good. And then he said he had to go back. I mean, I knew he wasn't going to be here forever, and maybe that's why talking was so easy. I knew I wouldn't have to deal with him, and my life would stay quiet. But then I was practically dragging him out of Vega's back to my house. My HOUSE! We had sex, lots of it. And we were less than responsible. And I didn't freak out until I woke up. I actually slept with him! Like sleeping, not just the sex 'sleeping together'." I was completely rambling at this point.

"So, you are freaking out over a few things, really," she said so plainly. "He knows your secrets, you had unprotected sex, and he is leaving. That's it, right? Am I missing anything?" I could only shake my head. "Only one of those things is cause for concern, and I am sure that it probably can be put to rest with a conversation. The other things you are worried about aren't even things to worry about. Collins, you are a beautiful, caring, successful twenty-six-year-old woman. Whatever happened to you in the past is just that, the past. It's time you quit running from it and start living your life. Obviously, I'm not saying you need to go live a life with Jayson, but you need to live outside of your protective bubble. He wants to see you again and see where it goes, let him. Don't write it off because he lives far away, or you are scared of being talked about. That's not being fair to either of you. I do think you need to talk to him about the sex part, otherwise things are good." Cecily was being so reasonable, which was making me feel both worse and better at the same time. I had been living my life in a bubble. I kept relationships at bay because I felt I needed protection. Why should I still care what other people said? The people I care about just want me to be happy, and that's all that should matter.

"Those extra two years you have on me have made you so wise," I teased. "You are right. I have been so distant for too long. I don't give two shits what people say about me. If you have a problem with me, call me. If you don't have my number, you don't matter enough to have a problem with me." Suddenly, all the confidence that I poured into all the other parts of my life had snuck into my heart. I think it got there through my vagina, but it was there. "Thank you." Nothing else needed to be said. Cecily just smiled and we devoured our food while we talked about nothing important at all. I could be happy or heartbroken, but I had made the choice to let either happen, and I was good with that choice. We finished breakfast and hugged our goodbyes. Before I started my car, I sent Jayson a quick message:

    Cadie: Let me know what time is good for you today. I'd like to talk.

I wasn't expecting a text back, so I tossed my phone in my purse. The drive home was quiet as I thought about what all of this could possibly mean. It wasn't like I had an instant boyfriend, I mean, we just met. I didn't know the first thing about having a relationship. Let alone how to have one with someone who lived on the clear other side of the country and was crazy famous. There was so much talking to do. Guys hate talking, though, right? I'm going to talk him right out of this before it even gets started.

When I flopped down on my bed, I was engulfed in Jayson. It was his cologne, sweat, everything that we had done the night before. It was just so much. I was half tempted to tear the sheets off the bed even though they had only been slept in twice. But I just couldn't do it. If he was going to leave, I needed to keep him with me as long as I could. He said he wasn't going to let go, and here I was already holding on.

I must have fallen asleep because the sound of the phone ringing made me jump out of my skin. I reached for the handset on the bedside table, "Hello?"

"Cadie, are you alright? You didn't text me back. Do you not really want to go?" I shook my head, trying to process who this was and what time it was. The radio dock said it was almost two. Shit, I slept for nearly three hours, and this was Jayson.

"Um, sorry. I think I fell asleep when I got home from breakfast."

"You don't need to make up an excuse." He sounded a little hurt.

"I wasn't ignoring you, honest. I would like to see you. We should talk." Jayson agreed and asked me to come on over. I needed a shower and some nerves first. "I can be there around five, if that's okay?"

"That's good, just promise you will actually show up." I laughed a little and hung up. And just like that, I went straight back in "first-date" mode. This wasn't a first date, but when it is with someone like Jayson Martinez, I think they will all be nerve wracking. First, I need to decide what to wear, that will help me get in the right mindset for this talk. Cadie was so much more comfortable in dresses than Miss/Coach Collins was, and I had a closet full of them that I didn't wear very often. Most of them were some kind of vintage or pin-up style, so I could make them casual or dressy with different shoes and hair. Comfort won out today, though, mostly because of my nerves. I selected a pale green sundress with thin straps that tied at the shoulders. Flat sandals with natural makeup and hair, just the casual look I needed to be cute but comfortable. I gathered up my keys and my courage and headed out. This was going to be the beginning or the end, but it was going to be decided tonight.

Chapter 9

After Tonight

As I pulled up to the apartment building Jayson was staying in, I called him to see what unit he was in. The first ring hadn't even finished when he answered with a very sexy hello. "Hey, I'm going to park in the garage and then come up. Are you in 601 or 602?" There were only two team apartments and I figured he had to be in one. He replied, "I'm in 601, but the garage is a little far, why don't I meet you there so you don't have to walk down the block alone." I just laughed a little because it was sweet that he thought I needed an escort from the garage down the block, but more so because I was actually in the building's garage. "You don't need to do that; I can ride in an elevator for seven floors without getting mugged. See you in a minute." I disconnected the call before he had time to respond. One more deep breath gave me the courage to get out of the car and head straight to his apartment.

Jayson pulled open the door and I nearly fell over. He was dressed in navy suit pants, a crisp white shirt, and a navy tie with thin red pinstripes. Everything down to his brown oxfords was immaculate. The only hint of the bad boy was the shaggy hair and the tattoos that peeked out onto his hands. His deep, rich baritone broke the silence, "Green is absolutely your best color, Coach Collins. You look incredible." The breath in his voice made me press my thighs together. It was already getting warm, and I hadn't even crossed the threshold.

"You look fantastic yourself, Mr. Martinez. It does seem you are a bit overdressed for a conversation." He was dressed for a very nice dinner or a business meeting, and not for the easy evening that I had envisioned.

Jayson smiled at me with that smile and said, "I figured you might need a little more convincing to give me a shot, so I thought we could have dinner. One of the guys told me about a place, and it just so happens that they had a table available." I'm sure the fact that it was Jayson Martinez asking made the table suddenly available. He didn't mention the name of the restaurant, but looking at him I suddenly became very conscious of my wardrobe choice. We were obviously going someplace nice, and I had very bare shoulders and flat sandals on.

"I don't know if I am dressed for the occasion, Jayson," I said as I looked down at my outfit. His hand reached out and tipped my chin up to look at him.

"Kitten, you are far more beautiful than any place I could take you to eat." He then pressed his lips to mine.

I think I floated in the apartment and over to the kitchen bar area. "We have some time before we need to leave, so I thought maybe we could have a glass of wine to go with the talk you need to have with me." There was some sarcasm in his voice, but it was still dripping with sex. I watched intently as he removed the cork from the bottle of wine. You could see his arms flex in his shirt. His biceps were so big, I think he could have given the bottle a squeeze and the cork would have just popped out. The pour in each glass was far more generous than it should have been, but I had the impression that it wasn't in an attempt to help me loosen my guard.

Picking up my glass, I raised it to him in a toast and took a small sip. I recognized it right away as a pomegranate wine from a place not too far from here. The wine is great, but dangerous. It's the kind that you can have way too much of without realizing you have gone too far. Small sips. Take it slow. I took my glass and wandered over to the windows. This apartment had the better view of the two on the floor, it looked right over the stadium. Letting out a deep breath, I relaxed and gazed down on the field. I sure loved that place. Before I got too lost in thought, my hair was brushed to one shoulder, and a warm kiss met the back of my neck. Jayson was running a finger along the top of my bodice across my back. "I'd love to know more about this storm, Kitten." The top of my tattoo was visible, but only the dark storm clouds and lightning were what he could see. There was a story there, but that was for another time.

Jayson walked us over to the large, L-shaped sofa, and I took a seat near the corner. Instinctively, I pulled one leg under me and turned my body so that he would need to sit a little farther away. "I think there are a few things we should talk about before I have too much wine." He looked at me with expectant eyes and waited for me to speak further. I didn't want this to be a super heavy conversation, so I said, "Do I need to go get a shot of penicillin after what happened last night? I'm never that careless." He barked out a laugh just as I hoped he would, even though it shouldn't be a laughing matter.

His answer was a simple, "No."

Good, I was able to breathe a little easier. "You don't either. You also don't need to worry about child support," I said with the same levity that I used before. He continued to watch me, not saying anything. I was the one who said we needed to talk, and he was letting me talk.

"Jayson, you need to understand that 'dating' hasn't been a big part of my life. I have a very quiet life that I enjoy. You have a job that takes you away for long periods of time, as well as one that causes a lot of people to be interested in your personal life. I am not going to pretend that whatever this could turn into is going to be easy. For some reason, though, I am willing to try 'not easy'."

That same smile that greeted me at the door flashed at me once again. "I was hoping you would say that. There are still some seats on my flight tomorrow morning, and I am sure we can get someone to move so that we can sit together."

Um, what? Seats on his flight? Terror and confusion crept over my face. "What do you mean, seats on your flight?" Now Jayson looked confused. We obviously had two very different ideas about what dating was going to look like. "Do you think I am going with you tomorrow?" I whispered in surprise.

"You just said you were willing to try. How is that supposed to happen with you thousands of miles away?" I couldn't believe what I was hearing. I took a log drink from my glass, followed by a deep breath. I needed to make sure this came out right.

"I value your desire to spend more time together, but there is absolutely no way that I am following you across the country tomorrow. We barely know one another. Besides, I have plans, and things here that I need to take care of. I don't want to spend my time alone in a hotel waiting for you." I registered the disappointment he felt from my comments.

"How else am I supposed to date you if you live here? I just thought you could spend some time with me at my place. Don't you have the summer off now? You can spend it with me in Rock Cliff. My place is nice. You can go shopping, or go to the club when I'm at practice. You can come to my games. Whatever you want." His words were almost a plea, but I wasn't going to give in.

"Look, Jayson, I appreciate what you are offering, but I'm not going. If this is something you aren't interested in pursuing anymore, I understand." I was standing by the time the last words escaped me in a whisper. Then, I felt his strong hand on my wrist again.

"Don't go, Kitten. Let's keep talking."

"If we are going to keep talking, you are going to have to stop calling me Kitten," I said with an exasperated sigh.

He smiled and said, "But you make the most adorable purring sound when you sleep. Just like a soft little kitten." My face got very hot and I slapped him playfully.

"Are you saying I snore? That is incredibly rude!"

He laughed harder and pulled me toward him. "I didn't say you snored, I said you purred like a kitten. It is incredibly sexy. I could listen to it all night. In fact, I think I listened for a few hours this morning. But if it bothers you that much, I will try and stop." Jayson was talking right against my neck and I shivered. He kissed me once again, right at the back of my neck, and I melted. I was ready to fall back and let him take me over when his phone vibrated and broke our contact. He didn't give it a look, instead he spoke into my neck again.

"It's time for dinner." We didn't resolve the situation, and now I had another problem. At least I wasn't alone with the new problem. As Jayson stood, I could see that his pants were much tighter than they had been when we sat down, and even then they had already been incredibly tight.

A Town Car waited at the curb as we exited the building. Jayson had placed his hand at the small of my back when we entered the elevator and even after I winced, he didn't remove it as we walked. He reached down to open the door for me with a big smile on his face. I saw the massive bouquet of roses on the seat as soon as the door was open. There were easily three dozen and they were absolutely beautiful. He handed them back to be when I sat down. "The flowers are lovely, Jayson, thank you." I was rewarded with a smile and a kiss on the cheek.

The car pulled up in front of one of the uniquely, out-of-place buildings that popped up around town. This one looked like an Egyptian temple and had lots of very different businesses in it. I was familiar with the restaurant on the top floor, though I didn't eat there often. The door was opened for us and we were quickly ushered to a back table. A few moments later Paolo, the chef, came out to greet us. He shook Jayson's hand and patted him on the shoulder as they exchanged introductions. Jayson then motioned to me and Pao took my hand and lifted it to his mouth with a kiss and a bow. Almost immediately he started laughing, as did I.

"It's wonderful to see you again, Miss Cadence. Even better to see you with such a handsome man." There was the blush again. Why did everyone need to embarrass me about a date? Probably because they had never seen me with one before.

"It is great to see you again, Paolo. Is it too much to ask to get your rice the old way with our dinner tonight?" He used to make the most incredible food for my grandpa, and this rice was second to none.

"Anything for you, Miss Cadence! Enjoy your wine and conversation and I will see you again before you leave" he said with a nod of his head as he disappeared back into the kitchen.

Jayson looked on our exchange with a very inquisitive look. "I have known Paolo since I was a little girl. He used to cook for my grandpa. You made a wonderful choice for dinner. Thank you." What I had offered didn't quell the confusion. In fact, I think it made things a little more confusing.

"You are quite the riddle, Miss Cadence. There is so much I need to know. I can tell there are things that you just haven't told me that are probably pretty significant. You say you have a quiet life, but it seems like you know a lot of people. You don't have the life of a small-town girl, but you do. I need more of you." Lifting his glass to me, he toasted to, "Being comfortable enough to share our secrets." I followed his gesture and took a long sip of my wine.

"Is there really no convincing you to come back to Raleigh with me tomorrow?" I shook my head in response. "Does that mean you won't come out at all, or just for now?" Each question was laced with anticipation.

"If things continue as they are between us, I will come out for a visit. I told you before that I have a life here. Just because everyone thinks people that work in schools have the whole summer off; doesn't mean we actually do. I still work, and I have plans with friends for a few different things. I will never be the woman who will abandon her life for a man. My friends, family, and job are all very important to me. Would you be willing to drop everything to stay here?" There was some irritation in my voice, but I don't think he caught it.

He knew I was right; it wasn't something he was willing to do—or capable of doing—so it wasn't fair to ask the same of me. "I've never dated anyone like you, Cadie. All of the women who are interested in me want the ball player. None of them would think twice about leaving their life to follow me around." His words and his tone were sad.

"It's obvious then that those are not really the kinds of people you should be dating. If you want more out of life, then you have to make changes. What is it they say about doing the same thing over and over expecting something different makes you crazy? Do you want something different?" I asked.

"I want you," Jayson spoke those three words with such conviction and desire, I nearly fainted from the heat. No matter how difficult this was going to be, I was now more determined than ever to really give this a try.

I had been staring so intently at Jayson that I didn't notice Paolo returning to the table with our food. His words cut through the passion in the air, "If you two are looking at each other like that before you eat my food, I had better get the fire department on the phone because this whole place is going to go up in flames!" he laughed heartily and left us to eat. As I had remembered, the food was fantastic, and so was the conversation.

Jayson finally started to share more about himself during dinner. "Once my parents realized that baseball could be a job for me, everything in our family changed. They were supportive before, but then they took things to the extreme. I'm grateful that they worked hard, but they did it for the wrong reasons. They showered me with praise and attention because they just knew it would pay off financially. My brothers and sister hate me for it. We don't really talk to this day. I have nieces and nephews I've never met because their parents are mad at me over things I couldn't control. I don't really blame them, though. My mom and dad were dead wrong in how they handled things. As soon as I signed my first big deal, they wanted new cars and the house paid off. Of course, I was foolish enough to do it. That only opened the flood gates. Next thing I knew, they both 'retired' and wanted to move to Florida. I bought them a house there, and when I handed over the keys, I let them know that their account at the Bank of Jayson was closed effective immediately. That went over as well as you could imagine. Not even two days later, pictures of me playing baseball as a kid were online, and my Little League jerseys were for sale online." I could see the hurt in his eyes, but he wasn't quite finished. "It was only a few months later that my then girlfriend started hinting around that maybe she should quit her job so that she could spend more time with me. If I just gave her a credit card, she could take care of everything at my house for me and I could focus on baseball. When that didn't work, she told me that we should probably get engaged so that we could live together properly. I didn't agree since I knew she really just wanted to be a stay-at-home fiancée. She loved what I could give her just like my parents. The big ring she had all picked out never came, and she left me for a teammate I thought was my friend. After all that, I didn't get serious with anyone. Probably not the best move for my reputation, but I just couldn't keep letting people in who were going to disappoint me." The big hero looked utterly defeated after his confessions.

I didn't really want this to be the end to our evening but if we were going to continue, I needed to lighten the mood. I took his hand and looked at him with all the sincerity I could manage. "Jayson, I'm not interested in your money or fame. I'm incredibly attracted to your smoking hot body. So as long as you keep working out like you do, we will be just fine." I couldn't even finish my sentence before the giggles started. He gave me a smile and shook his head.

"I guess it's good to know that my money doesn't matter to you. I will, however, use what I need to in order to keep you in my life. You are different, Cadie, and I need something different in my life."

We were nearing the end of the meal when Jayson stood and extended his hand to me. I stood up and he pulled me in close. There was music playing and so we danced. I closed my eyes and rested my head right over his heart. I can't describe how right this all felt. There we were, in the middle of the restaurant, having a moment that felt so private, but was being watched by everyone. The song ended and Jayson tilted me back just a fraction for a kiss. Paolo stuck his head out of the kitchen door and clapped. He waved us out the door with a wink and a smile.

The heat was palpable between us. There was a magnetic pull that drew us closer to one another. His hand held mine as we made our way back to his temporary home. I tried to swallow that bit down. Temporary. In the morning, he would be on a plane headed toward the other side of the country and to a life that I wasn't ready to jump into. Future Cadie needed to deal with that. Right-now Cadie was only interested in the connection and the heat.

While pulling at each other's clothes in a desperate plea for connection would have been the order for just about any date, it wasn't right for this one. We held hands as we rode up in the elevator, and he held his hand gently against my back as we walked inside. Only having exchanged glances and not words, the heat continued to build. There actually weren't even words that adequately expressed just what I was feeling.

I tried to keep myself in the moment because I knew that thinking about tomorrow was going to take away from this. The one thing that I continued to focus on was that Jayson kept physical contact with me as we moved. There was always at least one hand on me. He finally pulled me all the way into him. One hand gripped my hip while the other skimmed up the side of my dress and over my shoulder. His thumb traced over my lips, and then my jaw, as he looked deep in my eyes. He softly caressed my neck as his mouth met mine. So gentle at first, but the fire was building.

As we stood there and kissed, I took to removing his tie and the buttons of his shirt. Each button undone revealed more of his perfectly sculpted body. I let my hands touch his chest and then his abs. My fingers ran along each defined muscle. It just didn't seem possible that a mere man could feel this incredible. Having studied his immaculate outfit before we left for dinner, I knew there were two cufflinks standing in the way of me removing this shirt. He let me undo each before shedding his shirt. We moved in silence through the loft to the bedroom. Jayson scooped me up and placed me gently on the edge of the bed. He broke our kiss as he traveled the length of my body to my feet. Holding my ankle close to him, he undid one sandal and then the other. His hands once again caressed the curves of my legs and up to my hips. He urged me forward, and my feet touched the floor. I reached for his belt and as I did, he kicked his own shoes off. His slacks soon hit the floor, as well, and through his boxer briefs, I could see that he was feeling everything that I was.

Like a slow torture, he lowered the back zip of my dress. I could feel his breath on my neck as his lips just grazed the sensitive skin of my collarbone. His large hands lightly brushed the thin straps of my dress off my shoulders, and my dress floated to the floor. He then made good on his promise to kiss every inch of me. Every touch of his mouth on me was fire. I got lost in the heat and thought of nothing but how incredible the burn was. He must have spent an hour or more claiming every bit of my skin for himself. I could do nothing but absorb everything he gave me. Jayson's touch was everything. His movements were all deliberate. I must have drifted off to some other reality, because every sensation was heightened. Even the sweat that covered his chest felt like cool fire pressed against my back. His arms circled around me and he hugged me gently and kissed my head. "What did I do to deserve you? I must be dreaming, because there is no way you are real." He was partially right, though; this dream was ending as soon as we woke up. I didn't want to close my eyes because it would come too soon, but the weight of our reality pulled me down in a deep sleep.

Chapter 10

Daylight

I woke in the exact same position that I had fallen asleep, with Jayson holding me tight to his chest. He slept with a pained look on his face. I couldn't leave us like that. He needed to go home knowing that I was still in this with him. I smiled a little because I knew that there was one sure fire way to get a man to believe anything you say. Yep, every *Cosmo* article and everything you talk about with your friends is the absolute cure for whatever is bothering your man. My man. Jayson had claimed me last night, and now it was my turn.

The hand I held over his heart as we slept skimmed down his chest and abs. Before I made it too far, his rough hand pinned mine down. Jayson pulled me to lie on top of him as he whispered, "Not now. Let me hold on to you. Hold on to this. This is exactly what I need to remember before I have to leave." I placed a soft kiss on his chest and rested my head. Self-doubt tried to creep back in. Maybe now that he was really leaving, he was breaking away.

"You are thinking too loud. I might be leaving, but I'm not going anywhere. Now sleep a little more."

I was laying there for too long before I realized that he probably couldn't breathe. As I tried to move, he held me tighter. "Getting on that plane is going to be one of the hardest things I've ever done. I don't know what you have done to me, Cadence, but I don't want it to end." We stayed there for as long as we could. When we finally had to move, we did so in silence. I slipped my dress back on and buckled my sandals. He dressed in jeans and a white dress shirt, but instead of dress shoes, he put on a pair of black Vans. It was just enough bad boy peeking through the professional. I couldn't help but smile.

He locked the apartment from the inside, leaving the keys on the counter. This was it; he wasn't coming back here. When we got in the elevator, he hit the button for the lobby and then I hit the next one down for the garage. The doors opened at the lobby, but I held his hand tight and we went to the basement garage. In space 601 was my Cadillac CT5-V. He put his suitcase in the trunk, and then opened the passenger door for me. The driver's seat slid all the way back before he was able to get in. He started the car and backed out of the space. I tapped on the screen and asked for directions to the airport.

We drove in silence, and he parked in short-term parking. This wasn't a goodbye that could be done at the curb. I sat and waited for him to open my door and he offered me his hand. We walked hand in hand through the doors at the airport and toward the security line. The tears had already begun to well up in my eyes and I squeezed his hand tighter. He squeezed, too, being strong for me.

It was time to say goodbye and I was swallowed in his embrace. We kissed and held tight. He said very quietly in my ear, "I can't wait to see you again, Cadie. Hopefully you will be ready to tell me how you got into the secured garage."

Did he know? There is no way he could. I couldn't hold it in anymore, so I just said it. "Building owners have keys and codes." I kissed his cheek and he turned away and got in line. I just had to walk away because I couldn't sob here in the airport. The Valley heat hit me as soon as I was out the door and I ran to my car. I sat and cried for who knows how long. This was going to be so much harder than I thought it would be.

Chapter 11

When The Party's Over

It felt like I have been turned inside out. Four days. That's all it took. Everything I had held on to for so incredibly long was gone. The hardest part was the person I let it all go for was gone too. I was holding on to hope that as soon as he landed, he would call. I had shared a small fraction of a secret with him that nobody outside of my family knew. Not even Cecily. What I shared was something that was guarded more than my privacy. I have given him enough, and with what he knew now, he could find out the rest on his own. If he asked, I'd tell him. I just hope he asks.

I had ignored my phone since last night, choosing to focus on the time I had left with Jayson. I wasn't surprised to see the multitude of texts and alerts. Once I was back home I would sort through the mess. I just needed to get home during this break in my sobs. Before I got out of my car in the garage, I did a quick rundown of all of the alarm alerts on my phone. There had been two deliveries, one last night and one this morning. I opened the front door to two beautiful bouquets of flowers. The mass of roses from last night, as well as a basket of sunflowers. They did nothing but bring the tears right back. I placed them in the kitchen and continued my sob fest up to my bathroom. I was going to cry in the bath.

I ran the bathwater and responded to the various messages. The one from Jayson had come in just after he went through security.

Jayson: You are far too beautiful to cry like that. We will be together soon.

I could only reply with a crying emoji and a heart emoji. Cecily was just checking in on me, and I told her that we could talk later after I had finished crying. It took a long time for the tears to dry. I stayed in the bath far past the point of comfort, so I wrapped myself in my big robe and moved to the bed. As I laid my head on the pillow, I caught his cologne on the sheets. Tears that I didn't know I still had began to spill again.

I watched the clock, not knowing for certain just what time Jayson would land. I held tight to my phone and hoped. When it finally rang, I was shaking so bad I wasn't sure I could even answer. "Hello?"

"Cadie, are you okay? I have been so worried. If I would have known you would be so upset, I would have found a later flight. It killed me to leave you that way. Say something, tell me you are all right." There was concern in his voice, but it was soothing. After a few more deep breaths, I was finally able to talk.

"I can't lie to you and say that I'm fine. I had no idea just how hard that was going to be. It's only been a few days that we've been together." That's all I was able to get out before I started crying again.

"Please stop crying so we can talk. I am just as upset as you, trust me, but I couldn't risk walking through the airport with red eyes and snot running down my face." He was trying to make a joke, but it just made me feel worse because I was that red-faced mess. Thankfully, Jayson understood that I wasn't able to talk, so he just kept going. He told me about his flight, and the people who stopped him in the airport. He talked about how humid Raleigh felt after spending a few weeks here. He told me that he had tomorrow off before he had to rejoin the team, and that he wanted to video chat with me afterwards. Then, he told me to get in bed and close my eyes. I followed his instructions, listening only to his voice. Over the phone he tucked me in. I pulled "his" pillow up to my chest and took in a deep, relaxing breath. "Each night you spend alone in bed is one night closer to being in mine. Now close your eyes and rest, my Cadie. I will see you in the morning. Goodnight." The line went quiet and sleep took me over.

***

The simultaneous ringing of my phone and the doorbell woke me up with a start. It was Cecily just alerting me she was on her way in. She had the key and the code, so the doorbell was just a heads up. Every part of me was hurting. Still mentally and physically exhausted, I didn't know how I was going to be able to do it today. Lucky for me, I wasn't going to face the day alone. Ceci bounded up the stairs after a couple of minutes and jumped on my bed. "There is no way you are going to spend today crying in bed! I'm giving you ten minutes to get up and get your ass out to the pool. You are going to fix that tan, eat garbage food, have way too many drinks, and enjoy your friends." Cecily was half off the bed when she leapt at me, grabbing my arm. My hair was up in a messy bun, and I had an oversized shirt on that was off the shoulder. "Oh my goodness, Collins, you have a hickey!" She was poking me right at the nape of my neck.

"I do not! I…um…got hit with a baseball…" I thought to myself, really, Cadie, that's the best you could come up with?

"Well, there might have been balls flying at your face but not baseballs! Monkey man tag you anywhere else?" She started playfully lifting my covers in search of more. We both collapsed in a fit of giggles. She was right. Staying in bed wasn't going to make me feel better. It would probably make me feel worse. I got myself up, showered and rummaged around for a cute bathing suit.

Cecily had busied herself in the kitchen while I was getting ready. By the time I made it downstairs there were bowls of chips and salsa and a blender full of margaritas. Yeah, it was before 9 AM, but it was summer vacation and alcohol was going to make today easier. We took everything outside, and I took up residence in a lounge chair. Einstein bounded over to Ceci with a ball in his mouth, and she was kind enough to play with him until he wore himself out.

The doorbell didn't ring, but more friends appeared in my backyard. Nobody asked about Jayson (probably on Cecily's orders), we just enjoyed our summer morning. It wasn't quite noon, but I had already been in the pool a few times, and I was sufficiently buzzed. I was lying back on my chair when my phone chimed.

Jayson: I hope your today is better than yesterday. I stayed in bed too long. Can you talk?
Cadie: My friends came over to "play." I can sneak inside for a chat.

I hit send, and a moment later the phone was ringing with a video call. I answered as I walked inside. His beautiful smile greeted me as soon as the video connected. I smiled, too, as I walked to the kitchen. The light was good here for the call, and I could prop my phone up and lean on the counter. "You look so beautiful all sun-kissed and messy hair." I hadn't realized that my hair was such a mess and sunscreen hadn't been a thought either. I tried to smooth my hair down when he told me to stop. "I said you look beautiful. Stop trying to change that." I couldn't help but smile at him. "There is something I need to tell you, Cadie." Yep, here it goes. This is the I had a really good time, but I think it's better if we leave this now. I let out a long sigh that Jayson interrupted. "Does that sigh mean you have already seen it, or is there something else you are upset about?" I had no idea what Jayson was talking about me having possibly seen. "Someone took a picture of me at the airport yesterday. Well, I should say they took a picture of us. It doesn't show your face, but it is pretty obvious in the picture that you aren't a fan or a member of the organization." Stunned silence. I couldn't get a word out. "Sweetheart, like I said, your face isn't in the picture, and as of right now, that is the only one out there. The headline makes me look like an ass, but doesn't go any further. They didn't even speculate about who you are. In the article you are a poor girl I had a fling with during rehab." A huff of a laugh finally escaped me.

"Isn't that what I am, Jayson? You were here on a rehab assignment and we did have a fling."

"Cadence, don't you dare turn what we have into some sad fling. I was and still am ready for you to get your ass on a plane and move in with me. This photo and article mean nothing. I honestly didn't even know about it until my agent sent it my way. I'm only telling you about it because I need you to know that what they wrote isn't true. You are more than some fling. And I am going to do a better job of keeping things more private. I know how, I just didn't think I needed to in Fresno. This isn't going to happen again. I'm sorry." Jayson didn't need to apologize to me. Deep down I knew what I was doing even having a public dinner with a celebrity. People are curious and are going to talk. Cecily already convinced me that those people didn't matter, I just need to keep reminding myself.

"Thank you for telling me, Jayson. I'm not exactly upset, just surprised. While I had an idea that this sort of thing could happen, I never expected it so soon. And I can't say I will ever get used to it or like it, but I will do my best if it means I spend more time with you."

We talked a bit about what the rest of the week look liked for him and his upcoming schedule. He was going to be home for about a week, and then traveling for two. Then he had a week off because of the All-Star break. Okay, I can figure this out. The wheels were turning in my head when I heard and felt a slap that caused me to jump. Jayson started laughing immediately and Cecily apologized. She didn't realize I was on the phone. She assumed I was just sulking.

"A slap on the ass is up your alley?" he teased. "She's the worst! It's gonna leave a mark."

Cecily then shouted over the blender she had just started up, "But you know all about leaving a mark!" He had a puzzled look on his face, so I tilted the phone to show the hickey.

Jayson actually turned the shade of red that I usually did, and then apologized. "I'm sorry about that. Can you cover it? Where is your shirt now? It did sound a lot like bare skin she slapped. Am I missing out on an all-girl naked pool party? If so, I'm even more upset I had to leave," he said with a devious laugh. I picked up my phone and gave him a tour of the polka dot bikini I was wearing. Jayson responded with the appropriate number of catcalls and whistles, as well as a plea to let him see it in person. This was getting easier. We talked for a few more minutes before he told me to go enjoy the rest of the day with my friends. He would call me back tonight to tuck me in again.

"We can talk about this now, right?" Natalia asked. Cecily had shot her a look, but I was fine. "Cadie, he is seriously hot! He looked at you like you were the meal during dinner the other night. But by the looks of the bite he took out of you, I guess you must have been dessert!" My friends exploded in laughter and I blushed. "So that's why you were yanking him out the door? You needed to see how big of a bat he was swinging? And since you are so upset, he must have been pretty good at bat!" I sighed and took a long drink from my fresh margarita.

"It was better than good. It was earth-shattering. How was I not warned ahead of time that it could be like that? Jayson is definitely a major leaguer, and everyone else before him has been learning T-ball." I fanned myself with my hand and my friends all laughed. This was going to be difficult, but my friends were going to help me get through it. We chatted more and enjoyed the afternoon, but I already missed Jayson.

I had been rolling this idea around in my head since I talked to Jayson earlier. Now I knew I needed to do it. I was getting on a plane tonight to see him. If I was going to pull this off, I was going to need their help. One of the benefits of time zones and being on the west coast was being able to travel overnight. There is a flight leaving Fresno just after ten tonight. After a quick connection that I would have to run to make, I would arrive in Raleigh around eight thirty in the morning. I would be able to talk to Jayson before I left, and when we spoke in the morning we would be in the same city. I set to work on booking the flights, hotel, and car service, while Cecily, Natalia, and Mel picked out things for me to pack and cleaned up our party. Cecily said she would take me to the airport and stay at my place for the weekend with Einstein as long as she could drive my car. As long as everything stays on schedule, and the hotel was on his way home, I would be seeing him much sooner than either of us thought.

Chapter 12

When I Get You Alone

Afew minutes after eight, Jayson called. I sat back against my headboard so that he could see he was "tucking me in." I knew we wouldn't be able to have a long conversation since I needed to get to the airport, so I played sleepy. We talked for a few about how the rest of my girls' day went and about my plans for the weekend. He told me he was a little nervous about being back with the team, but that some of the guys were going to take him out after the game for dinner and drinks. I had to take that opportunity to tease him about them needing him to help get girls. He didn't really respond, so I'm sure it wasn't too far from the truth. Our conversation lasted a bit longer than I had planned, so I gave a yawn and he knew it was time to say goodnight. "One night closer to seeing each other," he said as he hung up. He had no idea.

So far, I was right on time. I did have to jog to catch my connection, but everything went smoothly, and I made it to the hotel by 9:30 AM. I was all checked in and settled on the bed when the phone rang. Even though I was exhausted, I was in a much better mood than I had been. Jayson even commented on how much better I sounded. I hope he didn't take that as me getting over the situation. In fact, what I was doing just might make it worse. The one part I hadn't thought about in this whole plan was the fact that I was going to have to fly home alone in a few days.

"What's on the schedule for today?" he asked in an upbeat tone. I figured I would be honest about what I was going to do, but leave out the part of where those things were occurring. "Nothing too big today. I'm a little stiff and I didn't sleep well last night, so I have a massage and then I hope I can take a nap. I'll probably just have dinner delivered and watch some TV. Any suggestions for something good to watch?" Of course, I already knew that the game was on at 4:05 and I would be watching intently.

"I'm not sure if it will be on in California, but I do know of a baseball game that might interest you."

I teased back, "Oh, really? Who's playing?" Jayson was confident in his reply that his game was going to make the highlight reel, and that even if I couldn't see it live, I would absolutely see him on SportsCenter tonight.

"I've had some recent practice going deep and scoring, so I think it is going to translate well." Geez, set my panties on fire over the phone, why don't you.

"I think you need to go take a cold shower and get to warm-ups, Mr. Martinez. I would hate for you to be late for your first day back at work." I was the one in need of the cold shower, so we said our goodbyes for now.

I thoroughly enjoyed my time at the spa. I was massaged, buffed, polished, and relaxed. I made it back up in time to order some food and enjoy the game. I have spent years watching these games. There was just something different about seeing it now. I was treated to many shots of Jayson on the field as they were focused on his return. I also got to see him bat in the first inning. I swear he looked right in the camera as if he were looking for me. Then, as he stepped into the batter's box, he rubbed the base of his neck in the same place I had my little bite. I'm sure I was just projecting again like I was when he looked at the camera. But when he did it again in the third and seventh innings, I knew there was more to it. This was probably just his ritual; baseball players are very superstitious. But that last at bat was somehow different. I saw him take a deep breath after the second pitch, and there was a visible change in his posture. I watched intently as he connected with the ball. The cameras followed as it sailed over the wall. I was jumping up and down with pure excitement. He said he was going to do it, and he did. Waiting a few more hours for him was going to be difficult. I sure hope I had been right about his plans for dinner. I couldn't help but send a text that he would see when he was back at his locker.

> *Cadie: Congratulations on the big hit. Enjoy celebrating tonight!*

For now, I will relax and wait for a call.

It was nearing ten when I was alerted to an incoming text.

> *Jayson: Thank you. I had some great motivation.*
> *Cadie: Whatever the motivation, you had an amazing game. Have some fun tonight.*
> *Jayson: We are already at the bar, so I'm not sure if I can call to tuck you in.*
> *Cadie: That's too bad, I put on something new for bed. (pic included)*
> *Jayson: Cadie, you are killing me! You should also warn me, the guys are desperate to know what has my attention right now and are looking over my shoulder.*
> *Cadie: Sorry! I thought you might enjoy a sneak peek.*
> *Jayson: Trust me, I enjoy it. I will probably enjoy it again when I get home.*
> *Cadie: Scoundrel!*
> *Jayson: You keep sending me pictures like that, and I'll fly the 3000 miles to see you tonight.*
> *Cadie: You don't need to get on a plane. I'm pretty sure you can just get on an elevator.*

Jayson: If there was a magic elevator to the west coast, I would know about it.
Cadie: I don't know about one to the west coast, but there is one to the fourth floor. (421)
Jayson: Wait, where are you?
Cadie: Well, I'm on the fourth floor of the Umstead. I hope you are in the bar downstairs.
Jayson: No, I'm not...now I'm in the elevator!

A soft knock at the door less than two minutes later caused me to jump. My stomach was filled with butterflies. A much more insistent knock followed before I even had the chance to get up. The door pushed back against me as soon as I flipped the lock. I would have fallen over if I hadn't been swallowed by the arms of my man.

"What are you doing here? How did you know where I was? Are you going to stay?" I didn't get the chance to answer any questions because his mouth was crashing down on mine. He backed me up toward the bed and pushed me down while bracing my fall. Jayson pulled back just a fraction to give me that dazzling smile. "You have no idea how happy I am to see you." I laughed a little as he pressed himself to me.

"I would say I have a little idea, but that isn't the adjective I would use to describe it."

"We can talk later. Right now, I need to take off what little you have on and bury myself inside you." He spoke to me very matter-of-factly, but I couldn't help but giggle. I went to work removing his tie and unbuttoning his shirt. Jayson's hands and mouth were everywhere. It was like he was relearning what I felt like. I savored every minute of it. Except it wasn't just a few minutes—but hours—that passed. How on Earth was he able to do that after the game he had tonight?

It was just after 1 AM when we took a breath to talk. "So, I think you can finally answer my questions now." Jayson was speaking softly into my hair. My head was on his shoulder and my fingers traced the ink on his chest.

95

As I exhaled, I said, "I was so upset when you left, I didn't want that to be what you remembered. I had to see you again. And I couldn't wait three weeks. I hope you don't mind."

His arms wrapped tighter, and he said, "You being here makes me so happy. I was serious when I asked you to come with me before. I was trying to figure out how to get even a few hours with you these next two weeks. But how did you know where I would be? Are you stalking me? Not that I would mind."

We laughed and I said, "I didn't know for certain where you would be. I had to assume that most of you live here, or in Rock Cliff, so this was a safe, neutral spot. Even if you weren't having dinner here, getting here wouldn't be a problem. Oh my God, your dinner! Did you leave everyone there?"

"When you said you were here, getting up from the bar and leaving the guys was a reflex. I don't give two shits about what they thought or what they did after I left. It's not like they needed me to pick up the check. And since we are talking about it, I guess you don't need me, too, either."

I tensed up a little at his comment. I knew this conversation was coming, but it didn't make it any easier to have. I just ripped the bandage off. "No, I suppose I don't. I will, however, let you from time to time. I am not sure how much you were able to learn from the little I gave you, but money isn't an issue for me."

Jayson asked, "Is it from the accident? I wasn't able to find much online about it."

"Honestly, I didn't get a dime from the accident. Everything I have is from the money and property my grandpa left me. He was the one who introduced me to baseball, and he even brought it to town. See, he didn't have any grandsons, so baby Cadence played catch with him. By the time I was starting high school, he had bought the team and started working on the stadium. In order to secure the location, he purchased several buildings, including the apartment you stayed in. Over the years he lost everything and gained it back several times. He died right after he sold the team. While a majority of the estate was split between my mom and her brother, each of us grandkids also got some. I also got the remaining shares in the team and the building. I continue to lease the fifth and sixth floors to the team for visiting players and the people they bring in to do promotional stuff. Everything I make from the lease of the rental is invested, and I live off my salary for the most part. You are the only person outside of my family who knows any of that."

There, I said it, now he knows everything.

"My little Cadie cat was technically my boss a few days ago? Sleeping with the boss...that's really hot!"

I slapped his chest and said, "Actually, no. I sold off the remaining shares two years ago when the affiliation changed. It's hard to enjoy the games when finances are involved. I have been a Ravens fan since they joined the league, so selling allowed me to stay one."

"Well, I guess it's a good thing your boyfriend is their star player. You just might get to see a championship ring up close." Boyfriend. He said boyfriend.

Jayson traced the lines of the tattoo that filled my back. "You know I need to know about this too. It seems so sad for a woman so full of life. Why the storm?" This was actually something that wasn't so much a secret in my life. All of my friends knew, and I told anyone who asked.

"I will say that I started on it not too long after the accident. I was in a pretty dark place, and I did feel like dark clouds followed me. The lightning came right after Papa died. That was for the storm that was still raging. Now it's more of a promise. A desire to catch lightning in a bottle, like my grandpa did when he risked everything on bringing a team to town. The last parts that have been added are the waves and the sunrise. The bright orange and yellow are breaking through the dark clouds. The new day will always come. I'll finish the water and the beach soon enough. It's a lot more hopeful than sad." Jayson's finger traced each part as I spoke.

"That story makes all of my tattoos seem stupid. And most of them are..."

I cut him off, "Not stupid. They all mean something even if the reason you got it feels a little silly now. Your throwing arm has flames, the other machinery. And then the beautiful statue of the avenging Archangel Michael, the original dark knight, on your back. See, those are all very meaningful."

He laughed a bit. "I didn't think you paid that close attention. If I'm being really honest, the back piece wasn't even what I wanted. I thought it would be cool to have Jason from the Argonauts since he had my name and was apparently a bad ass. The tattoo artist who did it could only find reference pictures of statues with their dicks out, and that wasn't going to happen! He really wanted to do a realism piece, so I let him do what he wanted in that same theme. It's a good thing, too, because I found out that Jason lost everything and then died by getting hit on the head. That would have been awful to carry around forever."

I had to laugh a little. I turned over and snuggled up to sleep. "Goodnight, my dark knight."

I woke to the sound of the shower just a few hours later. Jayson was going to have to get going for the game today. I wanted desperately to join him, but I knew that would probably make him late. Instead, I tried to be a little helpful. I fished his valet ticket out of his pocket and called down to have his car brought around. Jayson probably didn't want to leave in his wrinkled clothes from last night, so I also asked for them to bring up the small duffle that was hopefully in the car. The shower was off, and I lay listening intently for Jayson to emerge. The bathroom door opened at the same time the bell rang. I heard a laugh and a thank you, and then he appeared from around the corner.

Jayson clutched a towel around his waist as he kneeled down on the bed next to me. "Thank you for this," he whispered as he leaned forward to kiss me. I watched lazily from bed as he pulled on a pair of shorts and a t-shirt from his bag. "I'm sorry I have to leave so early. I need to get home and change before work. Come to the game tonight, we will have dinner after." It wasn't a question, but a command. He kissed my cheek and forehead and was out the door.

Chapter 13

Out Of My League

I spent most of the rest of the morning in bed catching up on much-needed rest. The travel and excitement of seeing Jayson again got me through yesterday, but I really needed a nap to feel normal again. Around noon, Jayson sent me a text that I would have a ticket at will-call and he would send a car for me so I would get to the correct entrance. He asked that I arrive early so that he could see me after warmups. That request melted me and made me a little nervous. I obviously wanted to see him, but I also wanted to keep this for us. Shaking my head, I knew I could easily be another fan on the wall waiting for an autograph, and that I could manage.

The car would arrive at three, so I really didn't need to rush. I enjoyed a long bath and took extra time to try and smooth my hair out. This humidity was not helping the situation. I finally settled on a pin-up-style ponytail that I could secure with a bandana. Now I just needed to hope that my makeup and hair wouldn't sweat off before I saw him. To complement my hair and makeup choice, I decided on casual jeans and a t-shirt for the game. I cuffed my jeans and tucked my shirt in tight. Feeling good about how I looked, I made my way down to where the car would be waiting. As soon as the lobby doors opened, I was hit with a wall of heat and humidity. I was used to it being hot, but add eight-five-percent humidity, and you realize instantly what a sauna feels like. Yeah, I wasn't going to look cute for long.

I had been to Raleigh plenty of times, but never in traffic like this. This rivaled rush hour in Los Angeles. The hotel wasn't very far from the stadium, but it took over an hour to arrive. It took another thirty minutes to get up to where I was to be dropped off. Once we pulled up to the curb, the driver said, "Miss Cadence, please wait a moment while I let the office know that we have arrived. They will come down to collect you." Collect me? I'm capable of picking up a ticket at a window. I suppose waiting in an air-conditioned car was better than standing in line, though. A few minutes later the door opened, and I was greeted by a nice young woman. She looked to be college-aged and had her brown hair pulled back in a casual ponytail. I also noticed that she was smart enough to be wearing shorts. It was so incredibly hot here. I don't know why I thought jeans would be comfortable.

"Miss Cadence, my name is Sarena, and if you'll follow me, I can show you to your seat and then take you over to where Mr. Martinez will be finishing up his warm-up. Can I get you something to drink?" Saying this was over the top wouldn't be accurate. This was way too much to even comprehend.

I did, however, remember my manners. As I fanned myself with my hand, I said, "Thank you. Right now, water would be fantastic. I am not used to this humidity." Immediately Sarena began typing away on her phone.

We walked up a few steps and she handed me a lanyard with what looked like a ticket attached to it. Another employee appeared seemingly out of nowhere the moment we walked in the building to hand me a bottle of water. Looking around I realized that this isn't a regular entrance.

There was something similar back home, but I don't think they did anything on this scale. One more set of doors, and we were back out in the heat, except this time we were looking at the field. It was beautifully manicured, and there were guys in the outfield stretching and playing catch. This was the baseball I loved. Sarena led me down what seemed like a million steps to seats right behind home plate. Literally the best seats in the house, and not fifteen feet away from Jayson when he was on the field. "When we get back, you can order food or anything else you might like for the evening. Are you ready to go see the end of the warm-up?" Sarena asked.

"Thank you again, this is lovely. Let's go look at some men in tight pants!" Luckily, she laughed a little because I couldn't do all-business all the time.

It was another long walk back up the stairs, and then back down again several sections over. It was hot and I was already melting. As we approached the wall, I could see him. He had been stretching and then had done a couple of quick jogs out and back. Our eyes met and he gave me that big smile. If I wasn't already red in the face from the walk, I was now. Sarena gestured for me to come over to where the players were signing things for the fans. Jayson had made his way to the end of the receiving line and was signing just about everything that was put in front of him. I needed to capture this, so I took out my phone and snapped a few pictures of him in his element. This is what he was made for. Everyone loved him, and they told him so. He looked really happy. The next thing I knew, he was standing right in front of me.

"Anything you want me to sign for you, Miss?" He was being very coy.

I sheepishly replied, "I'm sorry, I was just hoping to catch a glimpse up close. I didn't think about being able to get an autograph."

He took my hand and pressed a kiss to my knuckles, "Well, I hope this is satisfactory. Please enjoy the game this evening." Yeah, I was definitely blushing now. When he spoke to me, everyone else had disappeared. I could really get used to this.

Sarena walked me back to my seat, and to my surprise she stayed. I realized that Jayson didn't want me to have to sit alone, so he got me a babysitter. I wasn't mad because it was nice to have someone to talk to, even if it was pretty superficial. Throughout the game she was attentive without being annoying. Anything that I wanted, I got very quickly. The best part of the whole experience, though, was just how close I was to Jayson throughout the game. He was incredible. I watched him throw out players at second, catch a couple pop flies, and even hit another home run. This one had gone over the fence and into a tunnel. Usually someone was over there to toss it up into the stands. Instead, a few minutes later, I was handed a ball with a big scuff on it by another staff member. "Mr. Martinez wanted to make sure you got this." There was no way he could have managed that, could he? Sarena said with a giggle, "Maybe you can have him sign it after the game." I just smiled.

As the game was drawing to a close, Sarena let me know there would be some fireworks and that we should stay until the crowd had dispersed. I went along mostly because I wasn't exactly sure where to meet Jayson after the game. He never told me. We sat and enjoyed the show, and as soon as the aisle was cleared, I followed Sarena back up to the concourse. Instead of going back the way we came, we went through another hallway and down a ramp. We got to a door labeled clubhouse, and she said we would just need to wait another minute or two. The door opened, and there was Jayson freshly showered and in casual clothes. He dropped his bag and swept me up in a big hug.

When he put me down, I turned to thank Sarena for all that she had done and for her company, but she had already gone. I smiled up at Jayson and thanked him for the wonderful evening. "I am so glad you enjoyed yourself, Miss

Collins. Was everything to your liking?" His words were formal but playful.

I looked up at him through my lashes and said, "Tonight has been exceptional, Jayson. My boyfriend must be a pretty big deal to be able to coordinate it all. Everything was very thoughtful and appreciated. I was even given this ball after he hit a home run." Jayson took the ball from me, produced a pen from his pocket, and signed it with a #38.

"I sign and number all the home runs. This one was special because it was for you. It also happened to put me in the lead," he said with a wink. Jayson explained that there is always someone from the team who goes to collect the home run balls he hits to bring to him for signature. They take the ball back to the fan along with a few other things from him. How incredibly special.

I was grinning from ear to ear as Jayson and I walked hand in hand down the hall toward the parking area. I really shouldn't have been surprised to see the deep navy Bentley Continental GT parked in his assigned space. The car was almost as beautiful as the man driving it. He deposited his bag in the trunk and opened the door for me. After he got in, I asked if we could head back to my hotel so I could freshen up before dinner. Being outside all day had left me very sticky. I also wasn't dressed nearly as nice as Jayson was for dinner.

Jayson looked over at me and smiled. "I think you look beautiful just the way you are. And you won't be going back there. I took the liberty of having your things brought over to my house and checked you out. I hope you don't mind. Tonight, you are sleeping in my bed."

I suddenly felt very flush. "I think that will be perfect."

We held hands for the near hour drive back to his house as we talked about his game. The freeway turned into city streets, and then a more suburban area. Not that you could call Rock Cliff the suburbs, it was far too nice for that. The houses in his neighborhood were all tucked in away from the road. We drove up a long driveway to a beautiful ranch-style home. There was beautiful brickwork and a wraparound porch. It wasn't exactly the kind of house I pictured him living in, but it was stunning. He led me inside and I was even more surprised. While the outside looked like older construction, the interior had been completely renovated. There were exposed beams and slate floors. The kitchen was a chef's dream with state-of-the-art appliances. I wish I could have seen more, but he was pulling me rather quickly down the hall to the left to what was obviously his room.

The moment I crossed the threshold, he turned on me with a fire in his eyes. His hands were already unzipping my jeans as he said, "I didn't like you not coming home with me on Wednesday, Cadie. You need to be here with me. Now take your clothes off." Jayson was growling in the sexiest and scariest way imaginable. I didn't want to protest, but I did just a little.

"Jayson, I really want to take a shower before dinner"

"Then do as I say and take your clothes off." I didn't hesitate. I kicked off my shoes and socks, and was pulling at the hem of my shirt when he started helping. I guess I wasn't working fast enough for him. Our clothes were gone, and he scooped me over his shoulder. With a slap to my backside, he took us over to the massive shower. I slid down his giant frame as he turned the water on. It was ice cold at first, and the shock caused my nipples to harden immediately. Jayson took one in his mouth and nipped gently with his teeth, while his other hand squeezed my breast tight. My head fell back, and the cascading water rushed over us. His mouth made its way back up my neck to my ear. He pulled on my earlobe with his teeth and then said, "I'm going to fuck you hard and fast against the wall. Put your legs around my waist and hold on." His hands were under my ass lifting me as he backed me against the wall. I followed his every command, and with my legs and arms holding tight, he powered into me with one hard stroke.

"Fuck!" I called out. It hurt in the best way. He was still for only a second before he began his punishing rhythm. My body, slick from the water, slid up the tile with only a fraction of resistance. I felt one hand leave my ass and slide between us. His thumb made hard circles on my clit, urging me to the edge. I felt like I was on fire, and I desperately needed relief.

"Come with me, Cadie" was all I needed to hear to set off the explosion. Every muscle tensed in my body and I began to shiver. I felt myself clench down on his him, and I could feel the pulse inside of me. "Fuck. Cadie. Yes!" Jayson pressed me against the tile with his entire body and I melted. I could barely hang on, so he held me there. My head fell to his shoulder and I listened to his breathing slow. Mine fell into rhythm, and when I finally felt like I could stand again, I released the little grip I had.

Jayson continued to press me up against the wall for a few minutes more. He was taking deep breaths and centering himself like I did on so many occasions. This is the kind of rough and demanding I could handle. Shit, I would take this every day, forever.

Chapter 14

Howlin' For You

By the time we extracted ourselves from the shower, dinner had long passed. However, the late hour didn't make me any less hungry. Fixing something for us would only be a problem if he hadn't stocked his kitchen since returning home. But before food, I need to get dressed in something and figure out what to do with my now-wet hair. If I went to sleep with it wet, I would wake up looking like Medusa. The humidity here was nothing but annoying, to say the least. Even back home when I didn't really mess with it, I always made sure it was smooth or in a top knot. Here, both of those options left me looking like a frizz ball. Now's as good as time as any for Jayson to see what I really look like. I scrunched my curl cream through my hair, defining my ringlets. After fifteen minutes with the diffuser, the real Cadie looked back at me in the mirror. Okay, well, close enough. The secret of my natural brown hair was between Melanie and me.

Jayson had slipped out before I started messing with my hair, so after I dressed in a light sundress, I went searching for him. I turned the corner and spied him leaning up against the kitchen island. He was tapping on his phone when he suddenly looked up. Did he know I was staring at him? We made eye contact and he said, "True beauty." I could only breathe deep as he continued, "Most men could only dream of having someone as naturally beautiful in their bed as you, Cadence. Women wear makeup and do their hair to accentuate their looks. There is nothing you could do to make this anymore breathtaking. Only look like this." His words were burning into me along with his eyes. He had closed the space between us, and his fingers twisted a curl at my shoulder. The proximity set me fully ablaze. My hands slid up his chest and behind his neck so I could pull him down for a kiss. Even on my toes, he had to lean forward to meet me. Knowing where this was headed, he broke away. "I ordered some food. I hope you don't mind eating so late. It will be here shortly. Too quickly to properly finish what I want to get started," he smirked at me.

"Fine," I said very petulantly.

He walked me through more of the first floor. We passed through the open living area to a TV room. Well, it was a cross between that and a theater room. There were some oversized recliners, as well as a couple of overstuffed sofas. One wall was covered by a massive movie screen. The wall opposite of that was floor-to-ceiling shelving holding what had to be thousands of vinyl records. Sports memorabilia filled the rest of the space. A well-hidden projector apparently played everything. I really mean everything. Jayson had every game console on the market, every streaming service, as well as regular TV. Not just regular TV, but every channel that is available. I had to laugh a little. Who could possibly use all of that? I had a sneaking suspicion that there was really only one channel that he watched, and when he turned on the system my hunch was confirmed. Jayson flopped down on the end of the couch kicking his leg up as he turned on the TV. I moved to sit at the other end when he sat up quickly and grabbed my arm.

Jayson effortlessly tucked me against him like I was meant to be there. I snuggled against him as the highlights started. The lead was a story that interested us both. There he was stepping up to the plate and touching his shoulder. As if he knew that was what they would show, he leaned forward and kissed that same spot on me. The next thing we watched was the camera following the ball over the wall. The announcers talked about him overtaking another player for the most home runs, and that if he continued this pace, he could break a record. Jayson remained relaxed and focused on the statistics while his fingers twisted in my hair. The baseball recap was done, and they had started in on football training camps. This seemed to interest Jayson just as much as the baseball stuff. I was only interested in Jayson, though. The hand that I had rested on Jayson's knee was inching higher as my thoughts were lost to his confident strength. The doorbell drew us both back to reality, and I soon remembered just how hungry I was. Jayson got up to answer the door, telling me to stay put. I couldn't help but laugh a little when I heard a very enthusiastic, "Thank you so much, Mr. Martinez!" come from the very excited delivery kid. I'm sure the enthusiasm came from meeting Jayson, as well as the large tip that I am sure he received.

Over dinner we talked about everything and nothing. I was very curious about all the vinyl records, there were just so many. He told me that he really loves music, even though he never learned to play any instruments. "Records just have a unique sound that you can't get digitally." Jayson showed me his methodical system for organizing them too. Despite there being so many, he knew exactly where each was located, and had a story to go along with it. "I told you the first night I met you, Cadie, that you can learn a lot about a person based on their music. Every one of these records tells a story, and there is the perfect song to go with every life event." I could tell that he was really passionate about this. Maybe almost as passionate as he was about baseball.

"So, tell me, then, Mr. Martinez, what record would you put on right now?" I was hoping that maybe he was right, and I would get a glimpse into how I fit into this crazy life.

"That's an easy one," he said as he walked to the far end of the shelves. "The Black Keys *Brothers* album. There is one song on this record that says it all." I was a little surprised by his choice. But as I closed my eyes and listened, it made sense. He was saying so much with this. Now I needed to keep my fears at bay. Jayson was in this, and I needed to be too.

It wasn't until we were nearly finished easting that he asked when my flight was. He knew I wasn't going to stay, but I could tell in his voice that he didn't want me to go. I had chosen another red-eye flight so that I would be able to see him after the game. After a little compromise and coercion on his part, I agreed to change it to Monday morning so that I could spend one more full night with him, and Jayson could drop me off on the way to his own flight. It was now early Sunday morning and Jayson had to leave for work in just a few hours. This did not, however, keep him from giving me a full tour of his oversized, plush mattress.

When I finally woke, Jayson was gone. There was a note on the side table apologizing for not waking me, and asking for me to call as soon as I was awake. I didn't want to disturb him, and he was probably busy, so I sent a text:

> *Cadie: Waking up alone was a little unnerving. I guess I'll just snoop around your house until you get back tonight.*

Almost immediately, my phone rang. "There was absolutely no way I was waking the beauty who graced my bed when she looked so peaceful asleep. Feel free to snoop all you want. I would, however, prefer you come and sit with me at work. The car will be there in an hour. I hope you get in." Jayson spoke to me like he was reading from a fairytale. This whole thing did seem too good to be true. I wanted nothing more than to believe him, so I did. If Jayson wanted me at that game, then I would be there.

His sweet words gave me confidence, "Well, if my boyfriend went to as much trouble to make today as special as yesterday, then how could I possibly turn him down?"

I could hear his smile through the phone. "I was hoping you would say that. Please don't put a speck of makeup on and leave your sexy curls alone. Sarena will pick you up soon. I'll see you after warm-ups."

The phone disconnected and I immediately hurried to get myself ready. Jayson wanted no-fuss Cadie, and that's what he would get. I had a simple pair of denim shorts and a red tank top to go with my navy Chucks. I did tie my bandana around my hair, because no matter how hard I tried, the humidity was going to win that battle. I was just finishing up when a familiar voice called out from the kitchen, "Are you ready to go, Miss Cadie?" It was Sarena. I thought she worked for the team. Maybe she works for Jayson too? Oh God, could she be the bunny wrangler? I can just see it, "Go handle the chick I'm banging. Just make sure she is out of my house before I get home."

Nope, shake that shit off. Jayson has been wonderful. Not all guys are like that.

Now that my head was back on straight, I made my way back out to the kitchen. As I greeted Sarena, my eyes spotted a navy box with a pretty red bow on it. I know that wasn't on the counter when I was out here earlier, so I stepped closer for a peek. Sure enough, there was a small tag with "My Cadence" written on it. I smiled big as I pulled the ribbon free. The note inside said, "Getting one of my game worn jerseys tailored to fit takes longer than twelve hours, even with the best on job. Please consider this as a placeholder. It would mean a lot to me if you wear it today. – Jay" Inside was my very own Jayson Martinez jersey and a hat that I could pull my hair up through in a ponytail. See, Cadie, he was not one of those guys. I slipped the jersey over my shoulders and buttoned it up. It fit perfectly, and it was very cute. Having to leave tomorrow was quickly being erased from my thoughts.

Once again, Sarena was wonderful company. On the ride in we talked more about her job and school. She is a senior at Meredith College, and wants to be a social worker. Hmm, sounds a little familiar. Her job for the team is mostly VIP concierge, as well as promotions.

"So how did you get stuck babysitting me?" I asked.

"Are you kidding? I was ecstatic that I was chosen! Most of the time I just show people to their box and then spend the game keeping them happy with alcohol and food and their kids happy with every toy imaginable. Not only are you easy to be around, I get to watch the game! And Mr. Martinez is so nice."

I smiled and with a wink I said, "And very handsome too."

She attempted to stifle her giggle in an attempt to remain professional. "Well, that helps too."

I really like her! Hopefully I will get to see her again when I come back. I think I am going to be spending as much time here as possible.

We arrived at the stadium, and Sarena handed me another lanyard like the one I had on yesterday. I wasn't too sure why I needed one, because I literally didn't even use the bathroom alone. I did examine it a bit further and saw that I was in the same seat I was in yesterday. They are great seats; I wonder how they weren't already taken. Answering my unspoken question, Sarena said, "They are for team use. Usually, the owner gives them to a friend, or one of the guys asks for them so their families can sit there. As far as I know, this is the first time Mr. Martinez has asked for them, and since he is who he is, they had no problem letting him have them two days in a row." I mean, I knew he was a big deal, but not like that. Maybe it isn't as big of a thing as Sarena is making it out to be, though.

I asked if we could grab a couple waters because the heat was already getting to me, and we hadn't made it very far down the concourse yet. This time I made sure she had one too. I noticed yesterday that she wasn't ordering for herself when I did, so today I would take the liberty. We walked down one extra section today so that we were a bit more removed from the collection of fans on the wall. Jayson came jogging over right away. He had a brilliant smile that captivated me. Now he looks great in everything I have seen him in and out of, but in that uniform, he was so confident and relaxed that I didn't think there was anything sexier on Earth. Jayson reached up to take my hand. As he pressed his lips to my hand he said, "Hopefully you will let me kiss your soft lips before a game soon. But today I will have to settle for after." I wanted to lean over farther and give him just that, but the crowd of fans drew that thought away.

Through my flush, I said, "Thank you, Mr. Martinez. Have an amazing game!"

Jayson went down the line signing autographs and shaking hands, but called up to me as we were leaving, "#34 looks much better on you!" One more quick smile over my shoulder and I was headed back to my seat.

"I hope you don't mind, but I took a couple pictures, and I would love to share them with you," Sarena said guiltily.

"Really?!?" I was excited and absolutely terrified. I never considered that someone might snap a picture of us at the game. That was stupid on my part, considering that there are TV cameras and media all over this place. What if someone else got a picture? This time, they might be able to see my face. They might be able to identify me. I began to shake a little. Sarena looked like she was going to be sick. "I am so sorry, Miss Cadence. I will delete them right away. I didn't even think that you might not want your picture taken. Again, I apologize." Now I felt even worse. She was being thoughtful, and I had to be a jerk about it.

"No, Sarena, it's fine. I am still trying to get my head around all this, and I keep forgetting that people will take pictures of Jayson. Please share them with me. And I am sorry about my reaction. Like I said, this is all very new." She gave me a small smile and then started tapping on her phone. My phone notified me of an AirDrop, and I was pleasantly surprised to see over a dozen pictures of my interaction with Jayson. My favorite was him smiling up at me as his lips touched my hand. At that moment I had been so struck that I hadn't realized that my hand had covered my heart. It looked like a movie scene. I was dizzy with happiness. Once again, that fear that kept trying to bubble up was smothered.

This game was a lot closer than the day before. There was tension in the air, and I swear I held my breath every time a pitch came Jayson's way. His first at bat went well. A single and an RBI. The second at bat was very different. The pitcher was throwing him inside, and Jayson had fouled off three in a row. The last pitch looked like it skimmed his knee, and the umpire called, "Strike 3!" There was no way that was a strike. Jayson exploded. He yelled, and then in a fit of rage and strength, he broke the bat over his knee. My eyes followed him until he disappeared into the dugout. I couldn't see what happened next, but I heard it. There was a lot more yelling, and stuff was being thrown. My whole body was tense. I felt Sarena put her hand on my forearm and give it a gentle squeeze. "It's okay. They get upset sometimes. This one was justified. He will get over it. Why don't we go get a drink and sit in some air conditioning?" I sat still for a beat without replying. The inning was ending, and I waited for Jayson to reemerge. He kept his head down, solely focused on the field. The reassuring look I was waiting for never came.

I sighed and said, "Thank you. I think a little break is exactly what I need right now."

I hadn't planned on spending as much time up in the air-conditioned bar as we did, but his outburst had frightened me a little. I don't even really know why. It was a bad call, and I know that every at bat is important. But seeing just how angry he got, and how incredibly strong he is, was scary. I know how durable those bats are, but he snapped it like a twig. I swear it looked like he did it with his hands and that it was broken before it split over his knee. Deep down I know that isn't what happened, but it sure looked that way. Sarena's phone call brought me back to the present. I think I was listening as intently as she was. She said "okay" a few times and smiled at me. After she disconnected, I looked at her expectantly, and she let me know that we would head down just before the game was over to meet Jayson at the exit. I decided to sit and finish my second drink before we got going. By the time I was done, it was time to go.

We waited only a minute or two before the door opened and Jayson came bursting out. He didn't say anything; instead, he took my hand and pulled me down the long hall. I'm glad I had taken those two minutes to thank Sarena again because I was practically sprinting to keep up with Jayson. It wasn't until we reached his car that he pressed himself against me while backing me up against the trunk. His forehead was against mine and he took a deep breath in. We stood there completely still until I brushed my hand along his cheek and neck. Jayson finally spoke, "You shouldn't have had to see that. I'm sorry." I strained up on my toes to give him a kiss and to tell him it was going to be just fine. I hope he believed me, because I'm not all that sure that I did.

Our long drive home was very quiet. I was half afraid to talk and say the wrong thing. He was obviously not in a talking mood. It wasn't until we got back to his house that I realized that he hadn't showered and was wearing workout clothes. He really had gotten out of there quick. I hope that didn't mean an extra layer of trouble. I could assume that his outburst was going to cost him…I wondered just how much.

Jayson led me through the house and into the bathroom, and to my surprise started running a bath instead of the shower. It was a giant soaking tub with an edge that allowed for overflow. He stripped off his clothes rather quickly, so I followed suit. I watched as he stepped in the bath and saw the bruise that was already taking shape on his thigh. At least that answered my question of whether or not the bat broke before going over his knee, or because of it. Jayson had his eyes closed and his head tilted back before I even stepped in the water. My plan was to sit opposite of him, but he turned me to lean against him. His arms were over my shoulders and he was holding tight. Still, I refused to speak first.

"I get really angry sometimes. I don't even know how bad it is until it's all over. I really am sorry you had to see that. It was uncalled for."

Well, that was an understatement. He does sound contrite, so that helps. I didn't want to make it worse, but I wanted him to know that I was scared. I composed myself and said, "I am not going to lie to you and say it's okay. I don't know if it is ever okay to get that upset. In fact, it was crazy scary for me. I am a bit relieved to see the bruise on your thigh because I actually thought you might have broken the bat with just your hands, and that's terrifying." He held me tighter but laughed a little.

"I'm not that strong. My batting helmet and shelf might think otherwise, though. That was a very expensive at bat."

I didn't ask, but he offered, "At least ten." Yeah, that's a lot of money for a temper tantrum. I was very tense, and I knew he could feel it. "Cadie, I don't want you to be afraid of me. There is no way I would ever hurt you. Please believe that. I was so embarrassed with how I acted, I couldn't even look at you when I got back on the field. So, when I finally saw that you were gone, I was afraid you wouldn't come back. That's why I called and made sure you were at the door waiting for me. Just knowing that you were still around made me feel better. You make me feel better." Tears were already streaming down my face before his confession was over. Fuck, this is a lot to take in. I wasn't sure how to process it all or to even be sure of how to know for sure that Jayson wasn't going to get upset like that again. I just had to trust him. I had to take him at his word and let his actions speak for him.

We stayed in the bath far too long. By the time we had gotten to the soap, I was well past the prune stage. Jayson helped me out and wrapped a huge, fluffy towel around me. I sat at the vanity to brush out my hair, and Jayson stepped out to get dressed. I looked up in the mirror and saw him watching me. He was leaning against the door frame, shorts slung low on his hips and a shirt tossed over his shoulder. He didn't say anything, he just watched as I fussed with my hair. I finally gave up when he crossed the room toward me. The shirt he had been holding was soon pulled down over my head. No sexy nighties tonight, just quiet comfort. "If it's okay with you, we can just watch a movie and eat some leftovers from last night. Unless you want something else, I'll order whatever you want." Jayson's voice was lacking its normal confidence.

I really didn't want a weird night, so I decided to try and lighten the mood, "One fine and I am stuck eating leftovers? You know I can pay for dinner, right?" I was able to catch the subtle movement he made, and so I took off running toward the TV room. I probably didn't make it more than a few steps before he caught me and hoisted me over his shoulder.

"Cadie, how dare you! I'm suffering a financial disaster, and you joke about it," he said as he threw me down on the sofa. Jayson tickled me mercilessly until I could barely breathe. We laid on the couch together and made out like teenagers for hours. I fell asleep sometime before Loki opened up the portal, and I woke up the next morning wrapped in Jayson.

Saying goodbye was far from easy, but much less painful than the first time. My flight was leaving much later than Jayson's, but I had to go through security at the main airport, and he gets dropped off on the tarmac. The driver pulled up to the departure curb, and Jayson squeezed my hand tight. I was not expecting him to get out, but he did. Jayson took my bag from the trunk and set it on the curb. He reminded me that it was only nine short days until we could see each other again. I held tight soaking every last second in. It was time to go, so he lifted my chin and kissed me very gently on the lips. As he pulled away, he whispered, "Call me the minute you land in California. I need to know you are safe."

I held back the tears and ducked inside.

Chapter 15

Hot In HERRE

I was really surprised at just how quickly the days passed. We talked a few times a day, usually first thing in the morning and right before bed. The times weren't set because his schedule varied, but he never missed a call. It was almost time for the All-Star Break, and Jayson had been selected to the team. It was decided that he wouldn't play because the team didn't want him to risk injury. He would only participate in the homerun derby, and then he would have three days off in a row. My friends and I already had plans for part of that time, so I invited him to come out to my place. He agreed as long as we could have some alone time. Did he really think I wasn't going to be able to spend time with him alone? Just as I would never ditch my friends for a guy, they would never get in the way of me getting some.

Part of our summer traditions around this time is spending the Fourth of July at the ballpark. This is something that I have been doing since my grandpa brought the team here. Those first few years it took place at the local university, and now it is at their very own stadium. My friends, including all the spouses and any kids, enjoy every single treat at the park. We all eat way too much, get too much sun, and then when the game is over, we make our way down to the field and watch the fireworks. It is an incredibly long day, but it is so much fun. Cecily and I were both solo today so we sat together on a blanket near our friends. I was tired, so I was leaning my head over on Cecily when Derrick joined us. He pulled awkwardly on the grass next to the blanket. There was something he wanted to say to me, and I had a feeling I knew exactly what it was.

"Cadie, I know the last time we talked I was a little abrupt, but I just didn't want you to get tangled up in his mess. I knew he wasn't going to be here long, and I didn't want to see you get hurt. He is a known player and you deserve better." Well, maybe I didn't know what he was going to say. I was still irritated from the first time he tried to warn me off, and the lack of apology picked whatever scab that had formed right off.

I told him very plainly, "I will say it once more, who I choose to spend my time with is not your concern. I am a big girl and I can handle myself. I don't know what you have against Jayson, but he isn't at all what you think. If you aren't going to put whatever your feelings are aside, then it's going to be a long summer. I have..." My phone cut off my train of thought. It was Jayson, so I answered without a second thought.

"Hey, beautiful, have the fireworks started yet?" he asked sweetly. "Not quite yet. But there was about to be an explosion right before you called. Someone was offering up more unsolicited advice about my dating life, and I didn't appreciate it," I tattled.

"Well, put them on the phone and I will happily set them straight about your current status," he joked back. I had to laugh because if I handed Derrick the phone, his head would have exploded. Jayson continued, "I'm not going to keep you on any longer. Please call me when you get home. I need to tuck you in."

"Of course, there is nobody else I would want to give the honors to. I'll call you soon." Before I could say "goodnight" Cecily chimed in very loudly, "Goodnight, Jayson!" Derrick's eyes flew open and then scowled at us both. I hung up the phone just as he started getting loud.

"So, you actually fucked him? He's got you believing that he is interested in you. What now…you are going to wait by the phone and then spread your legs every time he flies over California? A guy like him isn't interested in you for anything other than getting off." I was glad that Ceci spoke up, because I was about to make a scene.

She spoke in a very hushed tone, "Do you even hear what you are saying, asshole? Cadie is a catch, and any guy would be lucky to be with her. It seems like you are the one with the problem, not Jayson. He would never speak to her the way you just did. You had also better hope that Cadie doesn't tell him what you said, because he wouldn't tolerate it either. None of us do! Get your head out of your ass or find yourself some new friends. Every one of us here supports Cadie in whatever she does. I've known her for years and she has never been this happy. Now you can apologize, or you can fuck all the way off. Choose now and choose wisely." Derrick chose to walk away. I hugged Cecily and we watched the fireworks without him.

As soon as I was back home and snuggled in bed, I called Jayson. He immediately changed it over to a video call and said, "I need to see you much more than I needed to hear you. Did everything work out after we hung up? Was the fireworks show fun?"

I am always really honest about my day when I talk to Jayson, so I told him what Derrick said and how Cecily told him off. I also saw just how mad he was getting as I spoke. "That piece of shit. I will pull his spine out through his asshole and then beat him to death with it. Or better yet, I can have him fired." I couldn't help but laugh at the visual. Jayson wasn't laughing.

"Jayson, he's not worth it. He was a peripheral friend anyway, and will not be missed by the group. By noon tomorrow he will have had his ass handed to him many times over. My friends are fiercely loyal to me and will always have my back," I explained.

"I know, Cadie, and I'm thankful for that. Otherwise, I would have to charter a plane to go and beat the brakes off of him. Then, I'd have to do it again because I would be mad about the fines and suspension I would face for kicking his ass in the first place. There is also the possibility of jail, and I am way too pretty to go to jail." We both laughed at that and then I yawned.

"Goodnight, sweetness. I will call you before warm-ups."

"Good-night, Jayson."

Before I knew it, Monday arrived and I was one day away from seeing Jayson. I was over-the-moon excited. Cecily was at my house, and we were preparing for our floating trip on Wednesday. Even though we were busy I couldn't help but check my watch every few minutes waiting for the home run derby to start. Once it was over, I knew Jayson would call. Ceci turned on the TV and we got to see the guys joking around during their warm-up. Jayson wouldn't have his phone on him, but I wanted to send him a text for luck.

Cadie: Thinking about you. Can't wait to watch you smash a few over the wall. Tomorrow we will celebrate your win.

My eyes must be playing tricks on me because just a few seconds after I hit send, I watched Jayson fish his phone out of his pocket and smile.

Jayson: Celebrating with you is the best incentive to win. Call you when I'm done showing these fools how it's done.

My smile was huge! Cecily smacked my leg to bring my attention back to the present. "You sure are love struck, aren't you?" she asked. It was pretty obvious that I was, and I had better turn it off before I scared him away.

"He sure is something," was all I could come up with. Something? Really? He was more than something. He was so much more than anything I'd ever had before. That's what scared me the most.

When we talked later a few hours later, he told me not to pick him up at the airport. I wanted to, because for once, picking someone up from the airport wasn't going to be a chore. He insisted so I didn't argue. It shouldn't have surprised me at all when the doorbell rang at 3 AM. There he was, gym bag slung over his shoulder, and full grin. I launched myself at him, not even concerned with the fact that my ass was hanging out on my front porch. He stepped inside, kicked the door closed, and ran up the stairs without putting me down. Having him home felt so good. I made sure he knew just how much I missed him, and how proud I was that he won the derby.

Einstein's barking finally woke us up way past my usual time. I apologized to Jayson because I knew he was tired. "Waking up with you is nothing to apologize for. I wouldn't care what time it was, as long as you were in bed next to me." Jayson's breath on my neck had Einstein waiting just a little longer. When we finally made our way downstairs, Einstein was fast asleep on Cecily's lap.

"Hot morning sex is no excuse to ignore your poor dog, Cadie," she joked. I was red in the face, and Jayson just strolled past us to the kitchen.

I looked at Ceci and asked, "Just how long have you been here?"

She couldn't help but laugh when she said, "Only a couple of minutes. You know this dog can basically take care of himself with all the crap you have set up for him. I think he needed a snuggle as much as you did. There is coffee in the kitchen, but I want food, too, so get on it." I gave her a salute and went into the kitchen where Jayson had wandered off to.

I handed Jayson one of the coffees Ceci had brought over and asked, "What do you want for breakfast, champ?"

Hold on, why were there three coffees? Cecily knew he was coming in early? My heart fluttered for my boyfriend and my best friend scheming to make me happy. Before Jayson could make a request, Ceci hopped up on one of the island stools and said, "You are making breakfast burritos. Get to it, Collins, I want fresh tortillas and everything!"

I cheerfully replied, "Anything for my two favorite people." As I bustled around the kitchen, we all talked. Neither one gave up any info on their planning, and I was okay with that. I noticed that Jayson watched me intently as I cooked. This was something I loved to do, and didn't get to do it often enough. Whenever I had company, I went all out. Thirty minutes later, I put plates in front of my guests with massive burritos and a bowl of fresh salsa. Jayson was done with his before I had finished wrapping mine, so I put mine on his plate and made myself another.

"How did it take me so long to find you? And how was it possible that you were single when I finally did? You are incredibly hot, kind, and an amazing cook. There should be a line of guys around the block waiting for a shot with you. You must be crazy, right? That has to be it. You are crazy," Jayson said confidently.

Cecily answered for me. "There is a possibility that she is a little crazy, but that really isn't why she has been single. Cadie doesn't waste her time on shit that isn't important. She is one of the few people I know who can be one-hundred percent certain about someone within ten minutes of meeting them. For her it's as simple as black and white. She lets you in, or you will always be on the outside. Cadie taught all of us that, and that is why we are so protective of her. She loves with her whole heart, and we love her for it." I smiled at my awesome bestie and then at Jayson.

He smiled and replied, "I am beginning to see just how lucky I am."

I couldn't help myself anymore. "You both are incredibly lucky. Now enough with all this nonsense, we have things to finish up before tomorrow.

Our annual float trip down the river was the grown-folk-only event of the summer. Everyone's kids stayed with babysitters, and us adults took to the river to relax. This year was going to be a little different because for the first time ever, I was going to be bringing a companion. We never started too early because the sun was needed to take the chill off the water. My SUV was packed, and so was Cecily's. Everyone assembled at the far bridge where we were taking off. With our stuff unpacked, Cecily and I left to take our vehicles to the spot where we get out with Natalia following. In the car I explained to Jayson, "This isn't like a lazy river at a resort. It's about a four-mile trip down to Cadie's Cay, and it's only one way. Ceci and I leave our cars here to drive everyone back when we are done. Then, we all go to my place for more food, drinks, and swimming."

Jayson asked, "Is Cadie's Cay where you took me the night we met?" It was. My grandpa named the little slice of beach that when I was really little. Of course, there was no coral reef, but the water was always clear and calm. I gave him a small smile and a shrug. "It is the back end of my sister's property now, so leaving the cars there is safe. Nobody else can get out there because there is no access."

We were back in ten minutes, and there was a very unwelcome interloper. I heard Matt shouting at Derrick before we even got out of the car. It was a good thing that Jayson came with me because I am sure there would have been a fight. As we got out, I reminded Jayson that he wasn't worth it, and the other guys would make him leave. He promised to only get involved if needed. Matt continued to shout at him, "Look, man, the guy has been nothing but cool, and it's obvious he is really into Cadie. She has made it pretty clear she isn't interested in you, and at this point, even if she was, none of us would let her near you. You are being an asshole with the way you talked to her and about her. Do yourself a favor and just leave. There is no more you involved in any of this, in case we all hadn't made that perfectly clear."

Derrick was pissed and had to try and get one more parting shot in, "Cadie, when he fucks you over, don't bother to come crawling to me for comfort." Jayson's whole body tensed, so I slipped my arms around his waist. My friends were handling it.

Cecily started in, "You are only trying to make yourself feel better by thinking she would have ever gone to you in the first place. The only reason she allowed you to hang around is because she loves that team. You have always been on the outside looking in. Now you lost that privilege. If you don't want to lose your job, too, get gone." He finally followed everyone's advice and left.

That wasn't how I wanted this fun day to start. "Thank you for handling that because there was no way I would have ended it without a physical fight."

Melanie's husband Bryan said, "We know, Cadie, and that's why we took care of it. By the time we would have been done with the cops, all the ice would have melted and the beer would be getting warm. None of us doubt your ability to completely beat the shit out of him, but I have a feeling big man wouldn't have let you do it alone." Jayson looked very amused.

"So, little Coach Collins is a brawler? That can't be true." Everyone started laughing immediately.

Mel slapped him on the shoulder and said, "You have no idea what you got yourself into with her. Be afraid."

The chatter continued as we readied everything down at the water. One more pass with the sunscreen, and we would be good to go. Jayson pulled his shirt off and there was a collective sigh. Cecily's sometimes boyfriend Trace said, "Christ, man, you are making us all look bad! Can you put that back on so we can at least pretend the wives are somewhat interested in us mere mortals?" Everyone laughed again, but Jayson moved to pull his shirt back on.

"Oh no, you don't," I said as I grabbed his shirt. "I don't get to see this everyday like the other girls do, don't deprive me because their men are scrawny." Jayson shook his head at me and smiled.

Melanie called out, "Let me know if you need any help rubbing in the sunscreen, Collins!" Her husband pulled her into the water with a big splash. My friends liked Jayson, and more importantly, accepted him. This was going to be a good day after all.

Back at my house that night, things got a little rowdy. All of the guys drank too much playing beer pong trying to outdo one another, and us girls just enjoyed the show. A lot of water got splashed out of my pool, and there was a heap of towels on the pool house floor. Jayson had gotten much more relaxed and flirtier as the evening wore on. He was constantly grabbing and tickling me. At one point, he had picked me up and tossed me down on the couch before falling on top of me. I batted him away, and he laughed heartily. Well after midnight everyone started to simmer down and retreat to their own areas in the house. Tonight was one of the night's that just about everyone stayed over. The only two who didn't stay were Matt and Natalia because they lived just down the street and could walk home. Jayson once again picked me up, but this time he carried me upstairs. We flopped down on the bed together. Very drunk Jayson was a lot like what I would imagine a teenage boy on prom night to be like. He fumbled with my clothes, and the words he got out clearly were more amusing than sexy. "Are you really going to have sex with me tonight? Because that would be awesome," he said as he dropped his head on my chest with a smile.

I sarcastically replied, "Now, Jayson, I don't want to take advantage of you in this state. It wouldn't be fair to you."

Playful Jayson was very clear when he said, "If you don't take advantage of me, I am going to be very disappointed."

That was all the affirmation that I needed, and I took full advantage.

Chapter 16

Closer

Whether was left of my summer just flew by. Jayson and I tried to see one another as much as possible. I would go there for a few days at a time, and he would sneak a day with me at my house here and there. I even went to a few road games for the night. Things were great between us. And even better, there were not more pictures of us floating around. He was always very careful with me in public. I think that was one of the things that made this so easy for me. What we had was just for us. Jayson's relationship wasn't what people were talking about when it came to him. It was all about baseball, and right now things with that were going really well. By now, it was looking like his season was going to go well into the fall. That was going to make things a bit more challenging for us. The summer was the really easy part because I didn't have to work. In less than a week, I would be back to work full-time, and our visits would only happen on the weekends for the next few months. We hadn't really talked about it, past Jayson telling me I didn't need to go back to work. Every time we got to that part of the conversation, I changed topics. The reality of the situation was stalking us, and I couldn't keep avoiding it. Well, I guess I could for a few more days.

For the last eight years, Cecily and I have attended a music festival in San Francisco to close out our summer. Each year we add a few friends, and this trip is no different. There were eight of us staying in an awesome rental I found across the bay on Lake Merritt. Sure, it was a lake in the middle of a big city, but it was beautiful. The house was also right by a BART station that could take us to the festival. The only thing that would have made this trip better was if Jayson was with me. I wasn't turning into that girl who can't do fun things without her boyfriend, I actually wanted him to experience it with me. This year's line-up couldn't be better. The nightly headliners included a Beatle, an Oscar winner, and the epitome of California rock. As much as I missed Jayson, I was determined to enjoy our end-of-summer bash.

It was just after midnight on Saturday morning when we finally got in from the first full day of the festival. I felt bad for calling so late, but I was used to our bedtime routine when we were apart. Jayson answered on the first ring, but sounded really tired. I wouldn't keep him long. He told me about the game and how well the team was doing. I already knew that because I spent at least thirty minutes every morning studying the box scores. While it had been my hope that the season would end early for him, it just wasn't going to happen. Jayson asked me who was headlining Saturday night, and I was so excited to talk about Nine Inch Nails. I've never seen them live before, and they were a band on my desert island list. Turns out that Jayson was a fan as well. It was late and time for me to let him go. "Goodnight, Jayson, I…hope you sleep well." I almost said it. I almost said those three words that would surely send him running. What was strange was that it was going to come out so honestly and effortlessly. I had to wait. Now wasn't the time for that.

Saturday at the festival has been amazing! My friends and I danced, drank way too many fourteen-dollar beers, and had too much sun. It was time for NIN, so we all made our way back to the VIP area for a much better view. We had stayed on the main grounds for the majority of the day just because we wanted to see all the stages. The extra we paid for VIP came in handy for the bathrooms and the headliner. Here we weren't all smashed together, and we had access to a bar with no line. I grabbed one more drink with Cecily as they started to play. The start of the set was an intoxicating lightshow with EDM that was so different from their more well-known industrial rock. All of the alcohol I had consumed in the sun, and the lack of water, had me a little off balance. The punishing rhythm of one of their most popular songs began, and I was entranced. Suddenly I felt arms snake around my waist. One hand was moving up between my breasts to my throat, and one was trying to get under my waistband. My heart was racing, and I started to panic. I did everything I could to pull away, but the attacker was too strong, and I was too drunk. The hand closed around my throat, and I felt breath in my ear. In time with the song, the man growled, "I want to fuck you like an animal. I want to feel you from the inside." It was Jayson. My heart was still pounding, but I relaxed a fraction. I tried to turn to see his face but he held on tighter. His hand slipped past my waistband and under my panties. His fingers slid along my slick folds, and he growled at me again, "This better be because of me." Jayson nipped at my ear and plunged his fingers inside. He fucked me right there with his fingers in the open along to the beat. I was dissolving against him. He kept me tight against his body, his hand putting just enough pressure on my neck to make it a little hard to breathe. Just as I began to tighten around his fingers, he let go, allowing me a full breath. The rush of air with the orgasm was like nothing I have ever experienced. I was hot, dizzy, and somehow invigorated. But just as sudden, the effects of the day were taking over. Jayson held on to my waist and said, "It's time to go, Cadie. You need to lie down." I tried to protest, but he was right. He turned himself around and had me hop up on his back. I held on as tight as I could, which wasn't very tight, as we made our way back to my friends. Jayson leaned over and said something to Cecily, and she nodded and then waved at us. I put my head down on Jayson's shoulder and he took us away.

I vaguely remember getting into a car that was waiting, and then riding in an elevator. It was the cold water raining down on me that helped wake me up. I was half standing in a shower with Jayson in what I could only assume was a hotel. Really, he was holding me up because I could barely stand. One arm held me tight against him, while the other worked soap along my curves. I did the best I could to not get in the way since I wasn't going to be much help. He finally sat me down on the small bench built into the wall and told me I needed to try and stay sitting up. Jayson washed my hair, and then took a minute to run soap over himself. How can guys get away with using the same soap all over themselves? I laughed a little at that, and it caught Jayson's eye. "I hope you aren't laughing at me because this is far from a funny situation, Cadie."

Drunk me thought, "Uh-oh, I'm in trouble now." Which of course made me laugh a little more. Jayson wasn't amused. He turned off the shower and wrapped a towel around his waist, and then sat me on the toilet. "I'm going to give you two minutes of privacy, and then you are going to bed." I hadn't realized how bad I needed to pee, and I appreciated his forethought. As soon as he heard the flush, he was back in the bathroom wrapping me up in a towel. Jayson snapped me up and walked out to the bedroom. He briskly dried me off and set me on the bed. I immediately fell over and relaxed on what was probably the most comfortable mattress I have ever felt. On the other side of the bed, Jayson pulled down the duvet. He scooted me over to that side so he could cover me, and then got in next to me. Once again, his arms wrapped around me and he spoke softly in my ear, "Cadence, I don't like seeing you this drunk. If I had known how drunk you were, I would not have taken advantage the way I did. That is never okay, even if you are my girlfriend.

That being said, you had better sober up, because having you naked in a hotel with only twelve hours to spare is killing me. Go to sleep." He kissed my hair and held me close. I was asleep before I processed what he said.

A loud thumping woke me. Oh, that's my head. I struggled to open my eyes. My mouth was sticky, and I needed the bathroom like immediately. I rolled out of bed and basically crawled toward the door. After I emptied my bladder, I practically stuck my head under the faucet to both drink and splash water on my face. Thankful to see a toothbrush, I took to ridding myself of hangover mouth. I drank what felt like another gallon of water from the faucet before I went to face my drunk shame. The old Sunday morning college prayer came back to me. "Lord, if you let me live, I will never get this drunk again." While I'm sure He had way bigger things to worry about, I still gave it a shot. I walked back to the main room not fully aware that I was still naked.

Jayson looked up and said, "Put that shirt on and then come have something to eat." Shit, he was mad at me. I slipped on the shirt that he had laid over the chair for me and made my way to him on the couch. He had ordered a lot of food, and I had no idea how long it had been there. Was I in the bathroom that long? I was going to take the chair across the small table from him when he patted the spot next to him on the couch and said, "They didn't have anything that resembled your hangover cure, so I got a few different options." I happily obliged and snuggled close to him. Jayson wrapped his arms around me and kissed the top of my head. This was my time to apologize.

"Jayson, I am really sorry. I don't ever do that. I could say it was because it was hot or it was because I missed you, but there really isn't an excuse." I tried my best to be contrite. I was sorry, and I don't really ever drink to excess. But I had tried to drown my sorrow a bit.

Jayson spoke quietly and calmly, "I am sure the hangover is punishment enough. But I can think of a few things that you can do to make it up to me." Thank God, he wasn't mad. "Now eat your breakfast and then we can have the shower that I wanted last night."

A full stomach definitely made me feel better, and it was time for that shower he promised. After spending too much time in the steam-filled bathroom, it was time to get moving. The only clothes I had were the gross things I had on from the day before. I wasn't interested in putting them back on, so Jayson told me to just put his shirt back on with a pair of his workout shorts. He was going to be dropping me off at our Airbnb, so I wasn't going to be seen other than the walk through the lobby, which wasn't going to be fun. The shorts were tied tight with the drawstring and then rolled over multiple times. I tied a knot in the back of the shirt, and I surprisingly looked okay. Jayson, on the other hand, looked like a Greek god. He was traveling directly to his game in Los Angeles, so he was suited up. He favored deep sapphire suits, and he looked incredible as always. The best description is a bad boy businessman. The tattoos on his hands, and his wild dark hair gave that suit an edge. Now I was embarrassed that he had to walk through the lobby with me. He didn't feel the same way because when the elevator doors opened, he held my hand and strode comfortably through the doors to the waiting car.

We drove over the Bay Bridge and into Oakland. In no time, we were parked at the curb in front of the house that held my friends. I had to say goodbye again. We said it a lot, but it was never easy. He took me up to the door and hugged me tight. "I'm not going to tell you not to drink today, but maybe take it easy. Even my chartered jet can't get here fast enough to save you tonight." He was only half teasing.

Then, it all hit me. "Wait, you chartered a plane to come see me yesterday? I knew you knew where I was, but tickets sold out months ago. How?" That was the only question that made sense.

Jayson laughed a little and said, "There are some advantages to being able to hit a baseball very far. I will use every one of them to spend time with you. Now go have fun and we will talk after my game. I will see you very soon." He kissed me with the passion that left me weak and breathless. I leaned against the front door as he jogged back to the waiting Town Car. I followed it with my eyes until it disappeared around the corner. There was a heaviness in my chest and a sadness that I wasn't used to feeling. But they didn't come from a place of hurt. Those feelings came from a place of longing. I wanted to be near Jayson. When we were apart, I missed him terribly. I might not be able to say it out loud, but I knew it was love.

Chapter 17

Arms of A Woman

I was so happy to be back at work. My students meant the world to me. Each day was a challenge and I loved it. This morning a beautiful basket of roses in my school colors was delivered to me. The entire staff of my school was also treated to coffee and bagels. Jayson is incredible. When we spoke later that night, he only wanted to talk about my day and all of the students. He listened to every detail and asked to know more. Each time I tried to ask about him he would say, "Your work is far more interesting than mine." I knew that wasn't completely true. His team was in the hunt for the playoffs, and Jayson was going to earn a home run title. I was excited for him, but regardless of what was happening with him, Jayson always made me the priority. We did talk about how we would make this work now that my schedule was a bit more constricted. I agreed that each weekend that he was home, I would go out to see him. Road weekends we would take on a case-by-case basis, and any off weekends he would come here. There weren't very many of those, so I knew I would be doing the most traveling. I didn't think of it as a hardship, because spending time with Jayson was important to me.

Our agreement meant that I would need to be getting on a plane in two days to see him. The logistics of travel planning was something I never liked. I knew Ceci would take care of my house and dog, and I could even count on her for airport transportation, but I didn't want to ask too much. Jayson took some of that off my plate by telling me he would send a car to drive me to work on Friday morning, and then it would take me to the airport right after work. I wouldn't arrive in Raleigh until very early morning on Saturday, but I should be able to get some sleep on the plane. Flights home from the east were easier since I would arrive not long after I left timewise. Maybe the logistics of it wouldn't be that bad. Getting to spend in-person time with Jayson was well worth any sleep I lost traveling.

As promised, when Friday morning came, a driver was waiting outside my house at six thirty to take me to work. I didn't want to hassle with a checked bag, so I just threw some stuff in my backpack and hoped Jayson wouldn't mind me leaving things at his house. He never gave me a "drawer" and I didn't know if it was too soon to ask, but the constant packing and unpacking was a chore. I was probably a little distracted during the day because I was mentally counting down the hours until I saw him. Sure, it had only been a week since we saw one another and we were on a video chat every day, but in person it is very different.

I was practically knocked off my feet when I saw that Jayson was standing in arrivals to greet me. It was just before 4 AM, and there he stood with flowers in hand. The airport was fairly quiet, and he had a different team's hat pulled down over his eyes, so he went undetected. As soon as I spotted him, I went running. I was three-thousand miles from my house, but he felt like home. "You look amazingly elementary school, Miss Collins," Jayson said, pointing out the paint on my shirt. I could only shrug as I looked at my paint-stained school shirt.

What happened when I got back to his place was nothing short of extraordinary. In what could only be described as mind-reading, Jayson had filled a couple of sections in his closet with clothes and shoes for me. His bathroom had all of "my things" in it. He hugged me from behind as I stood in shock. "I want to make coming here and being here easy so you will do it often. Cecily helped me make sure that everything is the right size and exactly what you like. If there is anything we missed, just tell me and I will get it. Next time, you only need to bring you. That's what I need." There was no way this was real. This kind of thing doesn't happen to me. I just had to tell myself to enjoy it while it lasts.

I was exhausted. A full week of work, followed by a seven-hour flight that I had promised myself I would sleep on, but couldn't, had done me in. It was two in the morning according to my clock, and that was way past bedtime. I sat on the edge of the bed and listened to the water fill the bath. It was going to be wonderful, if I could keep my eyes open long enough. I paused for what felt like just a moment. When I opened my eyes, Jayson was kneeling in front of me, untying my shoes and taking off my socks. He gently pulled my dirty t-shirt over my head and held his hand out for me to stand. I leaned on him as he took down my jeans and panties in one swipe. His fingers made quick work of my bra, and he took me in his arms, carrying me to the bath. I stepped into the warm water and sank down. Jayson undressed and slipped behind me in the water. I relaxed back on Jayson's muscular chest.

"Thank you, Jayson. For all this. It's really incredible."

His grip tightened. "Cadence, I told you I would use everything at my disposal to spend time with you. If having things here for you makes that easier, I will fill the whole closet. I need you here with me. We can talk about this later, but I want you to know that you don't have to go back if you don't want to."

I must be tired, because I think I heard Jayson ask me to move in with him. Not just move in, but quit my job and move across the country to live with him. I'm going to take the "talk about this later" clause and ignore this for now.

Jayson dried me off in one of his ginormous towels and laid me down on his bed. He got in next to me and snuggled me close to him. I was more than willing to submit to his every desire. But this time he wasn't after that. Instead, his fingers traced the curve of my breast and down my side. He felt my hip and my thigh and my stomach. My eyes were closed, and I was breathing deep. "I just need to touch your soft skin, Cadence. Go to sleep, love."

Too tired to think or respond, I fell asleep under the touch of the man I love. The man I think loves me back.

The alarm sounding behind Jayson came too early. Instead of turning it off, he held me closer. "I have to turn that off and get up, but I need this to last a little longer." He deep voice cut through the darkness of the room. Without releasing me, he moved across the bed and turned the alarm off. He made those moves so effortlessly, I forget how agile he is. Then, he did something else that reminded me. Jayson's hands were on my waist, and in one movement he turned and lifted me so that I was lying on top of him. My head was resting on his chest and I could hear his heartbeat. The slightest movement from my hands increased his heart rate. I also felt him twitch beneath me. My hand moved the length of his torso and he exhaled with a groan. With palms planted firmly on his chest, I pushed myself up and rocked my hips back. The testosterone that fueled his athleticism had him rock hard in an instant. With one motion, he buried himself to the hilt. I couldn't help but hiss in both pleasure and pain. I would never get used to this, not that I wanted to. Jayson pulled me down to his chest and said, "Waking up next to you is only bested by waking up inside of you." His deep voice sent shivers down my spine and my muscles clenched around him. He was guiding my body to move in slow, drawn-out motions. We were savoring every bit of this contact. One hand held my lower back tight against him while the other caressed the back of my neck, urging my mouth to his. This connection was like nothing I had ever felt with him before. I felt the heat building in both of us. I needed nothing else but to be in this moment and to release a powerful orgasm. Jayson responded to me by letting go with a deep growl. I was already fully pressed against his massive frame, but the crashing wave pushed me down harder. His hands held me to him to keep me from breaking our connection. I couldn't move, and I didn't want to. Here is exactly where I needed to be.

I peppered Jayson's chest with soft kisses as he contemplated getting out of bed. I knew he needed to get up for work, but I didn't want to let him go. "Now that you are up, I think you should shower and come to my game." I didn't have time to protest because Jayson was already sitting us up as he spoke. He stood up with me still attached. "But if I take you in there with me, I am going to be later than I already am. You get a little more sleep while I get moving," he said as he tossed me back on the bed. I couldn't argue with that, but instead of turning right to sleep, I watched Jayson walk confidently through the archway to the bathroom. Damn, I could watch him all day.

I must have fallen back asleep, because the next thing I knew, I was being pulled off the bed by my ankle. With a loud smack on my butt, Jayson said, "Get up, Cadie, I need to see you at my game, and more importantly, at the end of my warm-up. You have ninety minutes until Sarena gets here."

I curled up laughing, but I was able to squeak out a "Yes, sir!" complete with a salute.

"I'll see you in a couple hours. Wear the new jersey." He pressed a kiss to my forehead, and then my bare ass, before he left. I laid there just a bit longer and laughed.

When I extracted myself from the bed, I walked over to the closet. It was easily three times the size of mine at home, and was completely full. He had to have gotten rid of things to make room for me. The entire back wall was full of sneakers. There must have been two-hundred pairs. He also had a full section of dress shoes. There were suits and dress shirts, as well as more casual clothes. I'd never imagined a guy could have this much. The area that now housed my clothes was filled with a variety of choices as well. A zippered garment bag grabbed my attention. I peeked inside, and there was the jersey he mentioned. He had one of his game worn jerseys re-worked to my size. It was beautifully crafted, but you could tell it had, at one time, been a man's jersey. The appliques were all oversized and covered a majority of the front and back. I took it from the hanger and decided to pair it with some deep navy capri jeans. All I needed was underwear, and I'd be set. There were built-in drawers in the center island, so I figured that's where I would find what I needed. The top drawer was locked, so I moved down a drawer to find an entire selection of bras. The next was stocked full of matching panties. He really had thought of everything. They were all beautiful and perfectly my size. I made my selections and headed to the bathroom to get ready.

I had just finished tying my shoes when I heard that familiar voice call-out from the kitchen. Sarena was right on time and waiting for me. "It's great to see you again, Miss Cadence!" she said with enthusiasm. "The jersey came out so cute! I hope everything else is to your liking. I helped get it all organized in there. Mr. Martinez wanted to make sure everything was perfect for your arrival." I guess I knew that he would have needed a little more help than Ceci could have given by phone.

"It was definitely a wonderful surprise. It will make the back-and-forth travel that much easier. Thank you. I appreciate it, and I know that Jayson does as well." Sarena looked a little puzzled.

"I don't want to cross a line, but you said the travel back and forth. Does this mean you aren't staying here?" Wow, looks like Jayson isn't the only one who wants me to hang around.

"We haven't quite had that conversation yet." Sarena looked at me like she ate something bad.

"I am so sorry, I assumed..." I quickly let her off the hook.

"You didn't spoil anything. Just because we haven't talked about it doesn't mean it hasn't come up. He needs to spoil me a bit more before I make any decisions. Now, let's hurry because I can't miss warm-ups."

Once we arrived, things went much like they had the other times I had been here. Sarena led me down the same long aisle toward the field. I spotted Jayson immediately, and he smiled wide at me. He was already jogging over by the time we made it to the wall. "That jersey is very unique, Miss. It looks custom. You must be a big fan to have that made," he said with a smirk.

"It was a gift. My boyfriend is very thoughtful." I was blushing. Just as Jayson picked up my hand, his teammate, Jake Avery, came over and interrupted.

"Not like you to bring your workouts to a game, Martinez. Or have you not gotten in a sweat with this one yet?"

He was being a jerk, and since I'm not one to hold my tongue, I said, "I can only imagine it must be difficult for you to only manage enough stamina for a single game, especially when your teammate has the endurance for the game, as well as pre- and post-game workouts. He's a good teammate, obviously, so maybe he didn't want to embarrass you any further by showing off." Jayson smiled as he pressed his lips to my hand.

"Miss Collins, I cannot wait to kiss that smart mouth of yours after the game." I was immediately comforted by his words, and even more so when Avery jogged away. I hope I didn't go too far.

We sat and watched the game just like before. The one main difference was that Jayson made eye contact with me on multiple occasions. I even got a wink and a smile after he caught a foul ball just a few feet from me. He looked so happy in his element. I watched the game with a whole new set of eyes today. There was a new sense of pride I felt with every at bat and every play. Deep down I knew just what made it so different. I was really in love with Jayson. There was no sense in denying it anymore. I couldn't wait for the game to be over and to spend the evening with him. Let's hope he didn't make plans for us because I just needed to be with him.

We took our time walking down to the clubhouse door. As we walked, I saw a few players leave, thankfully none of them were the jerk from before. Just as Sarena said goodbye, the door opened. There he was, all dressed up with that panty-melting smile. He closed the space between us quickly and tugged me toward him. I felt his calloused hand on my neck as he leaned down for a kiss. This was the first time he kissed me where there was a good chance he would be seen by his teammates. "My Cadie Cat, with very sharp Cadie Claws. You managed to castrate my teammate and bolster my manhood with just a few words. I see now why your friends' step in ahead of you. There would be a trail of corpses in your wake otherwise. Melanie was right when she said I should be afraid." He was teasing me, and I got embarrassed.

"I'm sorry, Jayson, I should have kept my mouth shut. It was absolutely an occasion that I wish someone would have stepped in to keep me quiet. I don't want you to have any friction with your teammate."

A strong finger covered my lips. "What you said was far more kind than what I said later. I don't give a fuck if that clown is mad at me. He was out of line. The reason that he has never seen me with a woman at a game is because I haven't invited one in eight years. You are important to me, and I don't want to hide you, at least not from my friends. I will do my best to keep this private since it would create more of a challenge for you than me. Now let's go home and enjoy the rest of the night." We did my second favorite thing when we got home. I tucked myself up against Jayson on the big couch, and we watched a movie until I fell asleep.

A warm hand caressed my cheek, and I opened my eyes to see a beautiful man looking down at me. Jayson spoke softly, "Cadie, we have plans for brunch in less than two hours. I want to introduce you to a few friends." My obvious surprise turned to nerves instantly. I swallowed hard.

"So, no more bubble?"

"I told you yesterday I don't want to hide you from my friends. It isn't any different than me spending time with your friends. In fact, this will be way less scary because we will be at a restaurant." He was trying to be reassuring, but I got even more nervous. "Don't worry, we aren't going to IHOP. It is the restaurant at the golf club, and we will be in a private dining area. Very controlled. Now get up and get in the shower so that I can gawk at you while you are naked and wet."

I answered with a smile, "As long as you pick out something for me to wear. Otherwise, I will waste time trying on everything."

"I wouldn't typically be opposed to watching that either, but since we are on a schedule, I will oblige."

A beautiful emerald green dress lay on the center island of the closet. There was also his choice in undergarments. Everything was perfect, so I happily got dressed for brunch. I was reaching back to zip the dress when Jayson took over. "I will be much happier unzipping this later," he said before he walked over to his wall of suits. As he selected one of his many suits, I scanned the shelves for shoes. I landed on a pair of bronze strappy heels that would put me much closer to Jayson in height. I watched as Jayson opened a drawer in the island. It was filled with various cufflinks and watches. He pulled out a watch, a pair of cufflinks, and a small red box. Jayson spoke very nonchalantly as he walked toward me, "The one on your side is locked right now, but I'll put the app on your phone to unlock it, as well as the rest of the house. I would be honored if you would wear these today." The box opened to reveal a very delicate pair of diamond and emerald earrings.

I gasped, "Jayson, they are beautiful." If the earrings hadn't fully taken my breath away, his next words did.

"There is only one piece of jewelry that could make you more beautiful in my eyes. For now, I will have to settle for a little added decoration."

I gave him a soft kiss and said, "Thank you." He then tapped a few things on his phone and then opened the top drawer on "my side." I gasped as I saw watches, earrings, necklaces, and even bracelets. "Oh, Jayson, this is too much."

He wrapped his arms around me and said, "This isn't even close to being too much. All of these are just things. What's important to me is that you are happy here. If you don't like something, I'll send it back." I'm going to choose to believe that he knows this stuff doesn't matter to me.

"I don't want you to think you need to do all this to get me to love it here. You are the reason I love it here." Each time I said the word "love," he squeezed a little tighter. We were on the same page, but both unwilling to say it first. It was new, and we still had a lot to overcome. Meeting his friends and being a bit more public was the first step. I took a deep breath and willed myself to open up a bit more.

Brunch with his friends was wonderful. There were a few of his teammates, as well as his agent, who I think represented the other guys as well. The one person who just about had me starstruck…he was an actor who was on a show that I watched religiously with Cecily in college. I think he could tell I was a fan of the show, but didn't make me feel the least bit uncomfortable about it. Overall, brunch was private and relaxed. The players' wives, girlfriends, and I didn't have tons in common, but they were still nice to be around. I don't know if the whole full-time athlete wife/girlfriend thing is for me, but it seems to be working out just fine for them. I got a better glimpse into his life here in Raleigh. While I wasn't ready to make the move yet, I could definitely see myself here. I wonder just when I will be ready, if ever?

Chapter 18

Blinding Lights

It has been eight long weeks of travel and sleeplessness. I could see the light at the end of the tunnel. I was not quite sure how we managed to keep up the schedule and commitments that we made to each other. Without fail, we spoke on the phone twice a day when we were apart. The weekends, for me at least, were spent going to see him somewhere. He did come to me as often as his schedule allowed. He even made a few trips to see me when he could only be with me for a few hours. More than once he brought up me moving in full time, but he accepted that I wouldn't pack up and leave in the middle of the semester. The one thing that I think truly made this all possible was the fact that I retained my anonymity. If Jayson Martinez had a girlfriend, focus would change, and right now my mind needed to be on my work, and he had to concentrate on the playoffs.

Who were we kidding? Getting to the National League Championship Series was a breeze for Jayson and his team. He had set a single season home run record, and was playing better than he had in a long time. His performance bolstered the entire team. They had been so far ahead, and had been doing so well, that it wasn't a matter of if they would be there, but rather who they would be playing. Fortunately for me, the opponent happened to be one of the teams here in California, and Game 4 would be taking place on a Saturday in the Bay Area. What would make this game even better was if they won, they would be on their way to the World Series. So, Friday after work, Cecily and I would be taking the train to San Francisco, and I would get to wish Jayson good luck in person.

Somehow, Jayson was able to get an extra room at the hotel the team was staying in, and it was my intention that I would stay in it with Cecily for the night, and then stay Saturday with Jayson. My idea was dismissed immediately by Ceci when we were checking in.

"Do you honestly think either of you will sleep even for one minute knowing that you are in the same building and not in the same bed? I love you for wanting to keep me company, but seriously, Collins, I'll be more pissed than he will be if you try and stay with me." Just then, Jayson came striding through the lobby, flowers in hand. He was wearing a sapphire blue suit, with no tie. Absolutely beautiful. He handed a bouquet of sunflowers to Cecily with a kiss on the cheek, and then in the most dramatic fashion, swept me up and dipped me back for a less-than-publicly appropriate kiss. Cecily laughed and said, "And that's why you aren't staying with me, Cadie."

Trading my suitcase for the purple roses, he said, "Ha! Did you think you were going to be anywhere other than with me, Cadie?" Jayson was practically dragging me to the elevator now. He barked over his shoulder to Cecily, "We will see you for dinner in an hour. Make it an hour and a half." I only heard her whooping as the elevator door closed.

Jayson was ecstatic while in the elevator, and even in the hall for the most part. As soon as the door to the room opened, though, his entire demeanor changed. He was stalking me like a jungle cat as he followed me into the room.

He pulled me back on him as he collapsed on a chair. Jayson hugged me tighter and kissed my hair. "Cadie, you are incredible. Just having you here in my arms soothes all the rage inside. I have no doubts when I say that you are the reason I have played the way I have this half of the season. Knowing you will be there with me tomorrow is all I need to close it out so we can finish this season as soon as possible. Hang on a few more weeks, and then we can just enjoy us."

Of course, we spent a little time enjoying *us* before getting ready to meet up with our friends.

Dinner was late, but it was wonderful. A couple of Jayson's teammates joined us as we ate in a small dining room at the hotel. Cecily was her typical, carefree self. She was completely at ease with the situation and took every opportunity to share stories that always made me red in the face. Jayson held my hand, or had a hand on me the entire time. When we got back up to the room, Jayson made good on the promise he whispered in my ear during dinner to taste every inch of me. Every attempt to return the favor was thwarted. "Cadence, this is what I need right now. I'm re-memorizing you so that I can sleep peacefully and not think about any part of you I could have possibly forgotten about." He said those things with such conviction. It was complete sensory overload. There were not even words to describe this feeling. I remember Jayson sweeping the hair off my neck and pulling me tight against him. Then, we slept.

When the alarm sounded in the morning, we were in the exact same position as we were when we fell asleep. "Big game today, Mr. Martinez," I said as I wiggled up against him.

"Yes, Miss Collins, it is, and while I would love to distract myself in you, I have to get up." I made a pouty sound as he slipped from beneath the covers. "Save it all for the celebration tonight, Cadie. Because we will be celebrating, and you will need to be well rested," he said with a wink as he walked to the bathroom. I smiled like a fool as I looked up at the ceiling. Jayson emerged not even twenty minutes later, freshly shaven and smelling delicious. I watched greedily as he got dressed. Seeing him take off his clothes was amazing, but there was something fantastic about watching him cover up the bad boy. The thing is, he fits both of those things so well. He can be the perfect gentleman in the suit, and then the wild-eyed demon dressed in jeans. Neither of those held a candle to Jayson in his athleticism. Workout clothes or his uniform, both show off the man who drives him, all sides of him. "Cadie," he spoke in a very serious tone, and I sat up because this sounded serious. "I need you to stop eye fucking me because I really have to go. I'm sure nobody will want to sit next to me on the team bus if I've got a raging erection." I couldn't help but giggle at the admonishment. I sat up on my knees and kissed him once more before his big game. He reminded me of the tickets on the table, and that Cecily and I will be on our own in the stadium. One more kiss and he was out the door.

I didn't waste any more time in bed. I gave Ceci a call and told her she needed to start getting ready. We were going to take the train over to the stadium, and I had a feeling it would be crowded. Jayson had provided a couple shirts for Cecily to choose from, as well as a hat. He asked that I wear his jersey. He didn't need to ask, of course I would be wearing it. What I hadn't taken into consideration was just how outwardly nasty people would be to us once we made our way to the stadium. Seriously, I get it, we were rooting for the opposition, but we weren't playing the game ourselves. Saying awful shit to us wasn't going to change the outcome. We did our best to keep our heads down and our focus on us.

Our seats were in the first row along the right field side, and thankfully more like-minded fans were in that section. It also allowed us to be in our actual seats when Jayson came over to talk during the warm-up. We typically only said a few words to one another before the start of the game before he would give me a gallant kiss of the hand, and then step away to meet fans. I saw him jogging over, so I leaned forward in my seat, resting my arms on the short wall. "Looking good, Mr. Martinez!" I called out when he was still a few yards away. He gave me a big smile, and Cecily said, "Holy shit, that smile in that uniform...no wonder you chase him all over." Yeah, all that absolutely helped. He made it up to the wall and took my hand. "You look as beautiful as ever, Miss Collins." The heat was palpable.

"I wanted to wish you luck, Jayson. Have an amazing game." He pulled me a little closer and spoke just loud enough for me to hear.

"Cadie, when I told you that you are the reason I am here, I meant it. You mean the world to me. I love you." And in front of my best friend, and an entire section of fans, Jayson kissed me.

Before I could respond, he jogged away. I sat back shocked and flushed. The kiss was one thing, but he also said those words that I had been wanting to say myself for weeks. While nobody had heard that part, the kiss said enough. I vaguely recall hearing a few whistles and cheers, along with groans. I was in a hazy bubble. After what seemed like forever, I felt Ceci's hand on my shoulder and finally heard, "Collins! Are you okay?" Yes. No. My head was swimming.

"Is everyone staring?" My voice was shaking.

She patted my hand and didn't lie, "Well, a few people are. But that could be because you look like you are going to throw up. What do you need?"

I need to be able to breathe. I need to be able to form a sentence. I need my private life, private. I can say with one-hundred-percent certainty, that it isn't any longer. I would be completely shocked if nobody got a picture of what just happened. I took a steadying breath and said, "I'm good. Surprised, but good. Let's just get some food and enjoy the game." Cecily put her hand on my arm again and gave it a little squeeze.

"Cadie, don't lie. You are freaking out, but you don't need to. Your boyfriend kissed you in public. It isn't the first time it happened, and I'm sure it won't be the last. You know people do that all the time, right? That's as simple as it needs to be. He likes you and you like him. Just enjoy it. Now let's have too many beers and watch your impossibly hot boyfriend and his friends play their little game." And that is exactly why I love her so much. She was honest and sincere, and then made a joke of the whole thing to lighten the mood. I followed her plan and drank a few too many and watched what turned out to be an amazing game of baseball.

We waited quite a while for the crowd to disperse before we headed out. It was going to be a long trip back to the hotel regardless of how we got there. Things were pretty rowdy in the stadium, as well as the parking lot. There were some shouts and some name calling, just as there was when we came in. It couldn't be just that easy. Your team lost. Just go home. Again, we didn't play in the game. We were watching it just like they were, but someone always had to cross the line. I heard glass break, and my head got very hot all of a sudden. Cecily screamed as I stumbled forward, launching my cellphone across the asphalt. FUCK!

***

~Jayson~

I finally told my beautiful Cadence exactly how I felt, and I went into the game with the big dick energy that made me invincible. The only thing that kept me focused on this game was the fact that tonight I could look my Cadie in her eyes and tell her how much I love her while I'm buried inside of her. The sooner we won, the sooner I could make that happen. The innings were flying by, and it was finally the top of the ninth. Cadie was sitting down the first base line, so I was able to see her just a couple times this game. This last at bat I wouldn't get to see her at all because I had to go up left and my back would be to her. I got the signal just before I stepped out of the on-deck circle. We had runners on second and third, and any extra room we would give at home would help. Before I stepped in, I touched the base of my neck. It was my connection to Cadie. Kissing that spot on her drove her crazy, and that was all I needed. Cadie. This one is for Cadie. For us.

The new pitcher wasn't expecting me to bat left, so I had a bit of an advantage. He threw the other guys low and a bit inside. If I stretched just a bit, I could put one out of the park just past my Cadence. One pitch was all I needed. I saw it just as I thought it would come, and I hit it hard, sending it out for a splash landing. As I jogged around first, I saw my love cheering for me, and I couldn't help but smile. I was mobbed as soon as I crossed home plate. We still had one more out, and they would need four runs to beat us. That wasn't going to happen.

The last three outs came fast, and the team rushed the mound. We were headed to the World Series! We fucking celebrated right there on the field. They gave us NLCS hats and shirts, and that was just the beginning of the party. The clubhouse was draped in plastic, and the champagne rained down on everyone and everything. The team partied their asses off for over two hours after the game. The first bunch of us were on the bus back to the hotel when one of the managers stood up and told us that there was lots of press waiting when we got back. There had been a few problems in the parking lot after the game, and people got hurt. We all just needed to keep our heads down and get to the waiting elevators. I heard his words and my heart started pounding. I tore into my bag for my phone. I had too many calls and texts. I saw that the last three calls are from Cecily, not Cadie, and they all came in a span of about ten minutes. I listened to the messages she left, and now my heart was in my throat.

VM #1: Great game, Jayson! Cadie's phone isn't working, so call me back on mine.
Why didn't Cadie just call from Cecily's phone?
VM #2: Hey, Jayson, this is really important. Call me as soon as you get this.

Her voice sounds too worried. Why isn't it Cadie calling me?

VM #3: Jay, something happened after the game, and Cadie needs you. Fuck. I'll just send you a text.

I was standing and ready to jump as soon as the bus stopped. I need to get to Cadie. I need her to be all right.

Chapter 19

Hallelujah

I sat in one of the chairs in Cecily's room with my hands flat on the table. She was standing behind me holding a towel with ice against the back of my head. Some super glue, bandages, antibiotic ointment, and some Tylenol were delivered by Postmates over an hour ago. The hotel was nice enough to provide the alcohol I needed to fix the inside hurt, and Cecily had worked her magic on the outside ones. The knock on the door startled me and I jumped up a bit. Ceci hurried to the door, and it pushed open as soon as the latch was clear.

"Cadie, what happened? Where are you hurt? Why aren't you at the hospital? Who did this? I'm so sorry I didn't get here sooner." Jayson was speaking so fast while he picked me up to look me over. The color had drained from his face. I must look worse than I felt. Cecily could have told me I was a mess.

When he was finally done and holding my hands in his a little too tight, I said, "There was a minor altercation after the game. I have a good cut on the back of my head, and my hands are a bit scraped up. I'm not at the hospital because I'm not that hurt, and I also didn't want a dramatic scene if you saw me there. Cecily glued me back together, and vodka helped with the nerves." I tried to sound as calm as possible as I spoke. "Oh yeah, one more thing. I love you too. You ran away right after you said it, so I didn't get to say it back. And good game. But I guess we will talk about that later." Jayson took my face in his hands and pressed his mouth to mine.

Ceci laughed from behind Jayson, "And you said you didn't want some dramatic scene."

Jayson looked to her and said, "Cadie isn't telling me everything, is she?" Cecily shook her head, and I tried to cut her off with a "I'm sitting right here!" look, but she just started talking.

"No, she isn't. It actually started on the way to the game. There were people making rude comments and stuff. That, we could ignore. After your grand gesture, there was a bit more. It wasn't until we were in the parking lot that it got bad. Some drunk asshole made a really bad comment about you to Cadie, probably because of her jersey. She just kept walking, so he threw a bottle at her head. Then, it got super bad. Cadie fell forward and dropped her phone. I screamed because of the glass hitting Cadie, and the guy laughed. That didn't sit right with your girl because she hopped up and punched the guy square in the nose. The whole parking lot was pretty hectic, but we managed to get a cab and get here. I got lots of ice, and Cadie made the order for the things we needed. Also, I'm pretty sure if we waited around for help, we would be bailing Cadie out of jail and not waiting for her to be discharged." Jayson was pale and I was embarrassed.

"Ceci, you made that sound way more dramatic than it actually was." I needed to comfort Jayson with a little lie.

"Cadence, I need to know you are okay, and that we really shouldn't be at the hospital right now. Head injuries are serious. I can call the team doc and he will come to my room to have a look at you." His eyes were searching as he spoke softly to me.

"Love, I really will be just fine. I need a couple more Tylenol and a whole bunch of you. I'm sorry this ruins your celebratory plans." Jayson scooped me in his lap and rested his chin on my head.

"When I saw all the calls and the texts from Cecily, I almost lost it. If anyone had gotten in my way to see you, you wouldn't have been the only one knocking someone out today. Let's go to our room and I can take care of you."

Cecily held up the vodka and ice toward me and said, "Thank God! Now get out of my room with all that love bullshit. I need to get changed and get to the bar. I hear the hotel is full of baseball players celebrating something."

Jayson stood immediately with me in his arms and started walking to the door. He slowed briefly to pick up his bag, but never faltered with me. He thanked Cecily with a kiss on the cheek and told her, "Anyone but Jake Avery. He's an ass."

Jayson carried me down the hall to the elevator and didn't put me down until we were safe in our room. I walked to the bathroom to start the bath and caught a glimpse in the mirror. My hair was a mess, and I had blood streaked down my neck. My jersey was also ripped and stained with blood. That's what got me. I started to cry. I hadn't shed one tear over this until now. I carefully unbuttoned it and set it on the vanity. Hopefully it can be salvaged. I sat on the edge of the tub and took my shoes and socks off. I then realized how dirty I was. I was going to try and get some of this off before the bath. I turned the shower on and stripped the rest of my clothes off. Standing under the warm water both stung and felt amazing at the same time. I leaned forward against the tile and let the water rinse through my hair. Jayson stepped in behind me and began to part my hair, looking for the wound. With it neatly sectioned, he washed each part, trying to keep the shampoo from stinging. "You should have gone to the hospital for stitches," he said in a hushed voice.

"But there I wouldn't have gotten a shower with 'the' Jayson Martinez. I'd actually probably be sitting in the waiting room still. Did you really want to bust through the

ER threatening people like all the alpha males do in my naughty books?" I was teasing him, but that is the exact reason we didn't go. "I'm letting you play doctor tonight. Can that satisfy the caveman inside?" He wrapped his huge arms over my shoulders and laughed.

"Is that what you read about? Are we all that predictable? Because that is exactly what would have happened." I relaxed against his chest and sighed.

"Yes, big man. Every book. Every time. The man always comes bursting in to see his girl who has been hurt in some way, and then proclaims his love for her. But since you had already done that in a much more dramatic fashion, I figured that was another reason to skip the ER. The super glue from CVS also only cost like two bucks, and if I had a doctor apply it, it would have been like two thousand. How much do you charge for aftercare, Dr. Martinez?" He turned me around to look in my eyes.

"I'm very expensive. We will probably have to work out some kind of payment plan. It might take forever to pay back. You got that long?"

Forever. Yeah, I think forever might just work for me.

Jayson sat against the headboard of the oversized bed gently combing my hair as I sat wrapped in a fluffy robe. "I love how curly and unruly your hair is when you get out of the shower and when you wake up. You are a siren calling for me, and I can't help but answer. But you bring me to calm waters out of the violent sea. I am completely in love with you, Cadence. I don't want to ever see you hurting." He put the brush down next to me, then turned me around and lifted me up so I was straddling him. "Cadie, I have a big favor to ask of you. The Series is something that I have been dreaming of since I was a little boy. Now, I can't imagine it without you. I need you to be there when one of my dreams come true. Before you turn me down, hear me out." I nodded my head without interrupting. "While I would love more than anything to have you at every single game, that isn't really feasible or fair for you. So, I'd like to ask you to be at every game starting with four. Now, if by any chance we don't win the first three, then you can wait until five. I need you to be there with me when we win. Hopefully it won't be too much time away from work for you. I can talk to your principal if that would help. I just need you there."

I was smiling against his chest. "Jayson, of course, I will be there. I wouldn't miss it for the world. You don't need to write me a note to get out of school, I'm sure this is a pretty good reason for a personal day or two. Though, considering you just took out my principal's favorite team, she might not be as eager to agree." His arms tightened around me with questioning doubt. I had to giggle a bit. "You know I'm teasing you! There is no way that she would deny my request over that. I have the days, and I will take them. If I could take the whole two weeks off to be with you, I would. I know how important this is, and I hate that I will miss even one minute of it."

"Now that we have that settled, let me finish taking care of you, and then we can have dinner." We should be celebrating his big win, but instead he was brushing my hair and lightly kissing the scrapes on my palms. This comfort is exactly what makes all of this so right with us. We can burn with a fiery passion, and also enjoy the quiet intimacy of just caring for one another. These are the things that build relationships that last.

We had a quiet dinner in our room, enjoying the peace that had settled over us. It was nice to just enjoy being with one another. Just Cadie and Jayson cuddled on the couch like any other couple. Our bliss was interrupted when Jayson's phone started ringing. He let the first two calls roll over to voicemail, but when it started instantly ringing again, he picked up. I tried to scoot out of his embrace when he started listening more than talking, but he held tight. "Hold on a sec, let me put you on speaker because this has just as much to do with Cadence as it does me." My heart immediately leapt into my throat. Did someone know about what happened in the parking lot? No, this was about me and Jayson. Someone took another picture and was going to put it out there. The team's publicist confirmed my worst fear. There was a very clear shot of Jayson giving me a kiss before the game. This was not a fan photo. The local news station had recorded the entire interaction and had run it during the nightly news cast. They were only now asking for more information on "the girl." To say I was panicking would be an understatement. The same dread that had taken over in high school crept right back in. People who didn't know me or the situation were talking about me. Except this time, they were doing it on a much larger and more public scale. "Cadie, this is your call. I am fine with whatever you decide. We can say nothing and hope it is old news by morning, or they might go digging. We could also give them something in hopes they go away. Chances are, that won't be enough. I would love to tell you that you don't need to decide now, but we need to handle this, sweetheart." My mind was running through every possible scenario, and then worrying about all the ones I was possibly missing. I couldn't form words. The nice voice on the other end spoke up, giving us a work around. "How about I tell them that whoever the lucky lady is must be thrilled to have witnessed Jayson's game-winning home run, and that if he keeps up this hitting streak, he will be an obvious choice for World Series MVP. It makes it seem like we don't have information on who you are, or at least we aren't going to share what we know. It also turns the focus back to Jayson and to baseball. Since the sports guy is the one asking, I'm sure he isn't all that interested in the gossip part. But if Miss Cadence will be joining you for any games of the Series, you will probably want to have a plan as to what happens next. It was nice speaking with you both, and I look forward to meeting you in person, Miss Cadence." I wasn't able to say anything before she hung up. We did need to come up with some plan since Jayson and I were just about as serious as a couple could be before actually getting married. People were going to talk, but maybe this time I could control the message?

"Cadie, how about we keep things quiet until the end of the Series? If they ask me directly, I will steer things back to baseball. Once it is over, we can talk more. Will that ease your mind a bit?" I closed my eyes and gave a small nod. He hugged me tight and said, "Just know that I love you, Cadie, and very soon everyone is going to know I do. I want to show my girl off." He gave me one more kiss on the top of my head before carrying me back to bed.

Chapter 20

Wonderwall

It took eight days to finally know who the Series would be played against. I wasn't so much concerned with the ability of the team, but rather the location. The closer to home, the better. At least that is what I told myself. My prayers were answered when Seattle beat Boston. The more I thought about it, though, it really didn't matter because Jayson's home was across the country. There was a good chance I would have to travel that way anyway. I wanted it to be my home, too, but I just couldn't let myself think that way until there was a solid, legal commitment. Why that meant so much to me was really a mystery. Regardless of the paperwork, things could always change. People could always change their mind.

The first two games were played in Raleigh, and I was glued to the screen for every second of those two games. More than anything, I wanted to be there for Jayson. I think he did too. He wasn't on his game like he normally was. Midway through game two, Jayson struck out, and I caught another glimpse of the anger that could take over. Once again, he broke a bat and threw his helmet. I hated seeing those things because I didn't understand why he had such strong reactions to things that were really not all that important.

Our call that night was tense. I could hear in his voice that something was very wrong. He was distracted and upset, and I had no idea why. "Cadie, is there any way that you can come out to see me tomorrow? We will be here in Raleigh for another two days before we head to Seattle on Sunday. I really need to see you. I would come to you, but I can't." Jayson's words were a desperate plea. While it wasn't ideal, I could leave right after work since it was a Friday and spend the weekend with him.

"If I can find a flight after work, I will be there."

"I will handle the travel, just please say you will come." He was reaching out to me, and now it was hurting me that I couldn't be there to help him. I knew what I had to do, and that was make a difficult phone call to my principal to see if I could use up a week or so of personal days to go watch the World Series.

The conversation was much easier than I thought it would be. Since my job wasn't your typical classroom teacher job, I didn't have to plan for a substitute and I wasn't going to be leaving anyone hanging. I may have promised some signed items for the school carnival, but I would have gotten the time off regardless.

I was now an old pro at flying, and could sleep on the plane since I knew once I landed, I would be too wired seeing Jayson. Once I arrived in North Carolina, I made my way to the exit fully expecting to see a car waiting. I didn't expect to have Jayson waiting for me again! He wrapped his huge arms around me, and I felt a sense of relief. I could feel it on him too. We just stood there in silence for a few minutes before we walked toward the parking lot. "Just having you here has taken a huge weight off my shoulders. While I know I really only have one day with you, I am going to enjoy every second of you being here, and I will be looking forward to seeing you in just a few short days after that." Jayson spoke with such sincerity, I almost didn't tell him I was going to be with him all week. In fact, I didn't tell him until we made it back to the house.

I was tired from the trip, but I needed a shower before bed. Jayson was more than happy to join me underneath the massive waterfall spray. As his hands slid up my sides to cup my breasts, I looked over my shoulder to see his face was at peace. The tension that I had witnessed on TV and during our calls was gone. "Jayson?" I asked quietly.

"Mmmm," he murmured next to my ear.

"Jayson, I'm going to stay with you through the end of the Series. I made arrangements to take a few days off from school. I just need you to end this thing before next Sunday." He spun me around so quickly, I nearly fell.

Pure joy radiated off him. "Cadie, are you serious? You can stay the whole time?" He was backing me up against the tile as he spoke. Just as my back hit the cool white tile, he lifted my waist and pressed against me hard. "You are everything I need to stay focused and sane. You are the one who saves me from all the dark and rage in my head. I love you, Cadence, and I am going to spend forever proving that to you."

I was taken by his words. It gave me a chill and a spark of hope. Jayson was my home, even if it was thousands of miles from all that I knew. We kissed passionately under the flowing water, and I could feel the need building between us. "Forever, Cadie" were the sweet words whispered in my ear as he gently lowered my feet to the floor.

Waking up with Jayson's arms holding me close was the greatest feeling. I was warm, safe, and cared for. It felt like a dream every time I opened my eyes. How on Earth did I wind up with such an incredibly gorgeous man who was also so very loving and kind? One who was so different from the guy I saw on the gossip sites for all those years. I know it was my own insecurities that had me feeling that way, but damn it was hard to make sense of. "You are thinking way too hard this early in the morning, sweetness." Jayson's words were a whisper as his arms pulled me in even tighter. "Stop thinking and just be here with me for a bit longer."

We spent most of Saturday just sleeping, only getting up to eat and to pack Jayson's bag for the week. It was early on Sunday when we finally really got ourselves up. We needed to get ready to travel, and I was not looking forward to it. I was scheduled on another cross-country flight, and Jayson had to go with the team, which meant I was on my own. As I was packing up my travel bag, I heard the doorbell ring. Sarena's voice carried through the house, alerting us of her presence, most likely in an attempt to not literally catch Jayson with his pants down. She poked her head through the bedroom door and asked if we were close to being ready to go. Just as I let out a long sigh, she smiled. "So, I guess Jayson didn't tell you?" she asked with a furrowed brow.

I looked up from my travel case and said, "Tell me what?"

"I'm traveling with you! You know Jayson is going to be on the team plane and busy on the field, so he thought you could use the company." Sarena was absolutely giddy.

"But don't you have school?" I asked.

"I could say the same for you, Miss Collins. My professors completely understand. All it took was a couple of signed baseballs and some shirts, and I got a free pass. What good is putting up with Mr. Baseball if I don't get at least some perks. Now, finish up, we have a flight to catch."

Having Sarena with me was a blessing. It wasn't the same as having Cecily with me, but it was a close second. I was a bundle of nerves for Jayson, and I knew that wasn't going to help him in the slightest. During the flight, Sarena and I talked like we had been friends forever. While we had spent a good deal of time together, we never really had any in-depth conversations. She asked a lot of questions about my family and if I was close to them. I partly wondered if she was trying to see if they were the reason, I wasn't ready to move in with Jayson. I loved my family, and they were absolutely one of the reasons I was so hesitant. I was also terrified of being dropped as soon as he got bored of me. What would happen if I walked away from my life and moved across the country? That thought was always in the back of my head. No matter what he showed me when we were together, I still had that doubt that all of this was going to be over and I would be left in pieces.

"Do you really not see just how crazy Jayson is about you? I mean, really, Cadie, he wants to show you off to the world. He doesn't shy away from telling you how much you mean to him. As long as I have been around, he has never acted this way. Even his friends have seen how you have affected him. Stop holding back and let him all the way in." Sarena spoke with true emotion as she held my hand. I knew the words were true, but I doubted myself in a way that Jayson never did.

***

Game three was a blowout. Jayson was back in his typical form and had even hit another home run. I watched that game with pride, and even got a little teary-eyed when I saw him touch his shoulder, which was a nod to me. A reminder of that spot on my neck that made me melt. The Jayson who was out on that field was not the same man who had been pleading with me to join him for the weekend just a few days ago. I really did change something in Jayson. I needed to let him change that scared part in me. The part that I had let control me for so long. It was a piece of gossip from my past that controlled me. I didn't want to be gossip fodder again, and that is why I always held back. Maybe even more so from Jayson because his life was so public. It was time to accept that if I really loved Jayson, that was going to be a part of my life.

That part of me wanted to run, but all that went away the minute Jayson walked through the door of our hotel room after the game. He looked like a little boy at Christmas. He was as happy to see me waiting there as he was about winning the game. They were just one win away from the World Series title, and while I know a home win would mean the world to him, I really wanted this whole thing to be over.

Jayson practically tackled me back on to the bed. As he hovered over me, he took my face in his big hands and stared deep into my eyes. "I told you before that you are the reason that I play well when I do. Just knowing you are near makes things so much better for me. I need that in my life forever. I want to marry you, Cadie. I want to marry you and be able to thank you for the rest of my life for saving me from myself." I stared back and my lips parted. I could barely breathe, and it had nothing to do with the man lying on me. It was his words and the sincerity behind them. But this wasn't a proposal, it was a declaration. Fortunately, his mouth came crashing down on mine and I didn't have to respond to his words.

His rough kiss turned much softer as his mouth made a sweep across my jaw to my ear. His deep voice sent a chill through my entire body as he whispered, "The future Mrs. Martinez will get the romantic proposal she deserves, as well as a ring to rival the one she is helping me win. Just know it's happening soon, Cadie." Jayson's words melted me into the bed. Just like so many times before, he took his sweet time with me removing my clothes and worshiping every inch of my skin. This was his release. I was the panacea he needed to soothe the black spots. Even more, he was that for me. I knew that no matter what, I was safe there and he would make sure that everything was going to be okay.

The morning of game four and possibly the end of the Series came just a few short hours after we finally drifted off to sleep. Jayson woke when the alarm rang and hopped out of bed like a man on a mission. He was laser-focused on getting ready for the game. Breakfast was brought up to the room by a member of the organization, and Jayson ate in quiet. As he was getting ready to leave, he pulled me in close, looking right in my eyes again. "This is it, Cadie. I've been waiting for this for a very long time, and I couldn't be happier that you are sharing it with me. I will see you in our spot before the game." And with those words, he gave me a quick kiss, picked up his bag, and headed out the door.

An hour later, Sarena came up to get me. I was dressed and ready to go when she arrived. I was wearing the new jersey that Jayson had made for me just for this game. This time when I slipped the Martinez name on my back, it meant so much more. One day that would be my last name, and maybe that day would be very soon.

We walked out of the hotel to the waiting car, and I think that is when I started to hold my breath. Everything that happened after that was a blur. I got my credentials when we arrived, I saw Jayson like I always did. He gave me a kiss. We watched the game. I caught a smile here and there. Another ball flew over the fence. And then there was explosions lighting up the sky.

That was it. The game was over, and it was pure, celebratory chaos. Sarena held tight to my hand reminding me to stay right where we were because that is where Jayson could find me. It felt like forever when I finally saw Jayson push through the crowd. He ran right up to the wall and I leaned over to him. Without hesitation, he pulled me over and into his arms. Jayson pressed his mouth to mine and kissed me through his smile. "I fucking did it, Cadence!" Pride radiated off of him.

"I love you, Jayson!" was all I could squeak out over the crowd noise.

As quick as he was there, he was being pulled back away. Before he let me go, he lifted me back up over the wall and gave me strict instructions not to move until someone came back for me. Within just a few minutes, a stage had appeared in the middle of the outfield and the fans that had rushed on the field were being ushered back behind ropes. It was so incredibly loud that I didn't even know if I was hearing clearly when Jayson was called up by name.

Sarena had been holding my hand tight and shouted to me, "This is big Cadie, try and listen." I was holding my breath as Jayson was being talked to on stage.

"Jayson, you have had an incredible season since returning from your injury. I don't think it is any surprise that you are this year's World Series MVP. What do you have to say?"

"I couldn't have done any of this without the support of the amazing people in my life. It has been a long road, but one I would happily travel again if I was guaranteed the same outcome."

"Now for the part that every player dreams about getting to say. Jayson Martinez, you and the Raleigh Ravens have just won the World Series...what are you going to do next?"

"I'm going to take my beautiful girlfriend Cadence on a trip to Disneyland!"

I was in utter and complete shock. First the Series, and then he said it out loud in front of millions. My life was about to get very complicated. I wasn't scared in the slightest, though. I was overflowing with joy, and it was taking everything I had to stay still and not run to him. I couldn't get lost in the crowd. Thank God Sarena was holding on tight because my knees were weak and people were starting to push toward us. I closed my eyes, took a deep breath, and waited to be reunited with Jayson.

Chapter 21

In Your Eyes

As I had imagined, things got a little crazy for me when I got home. It only took a couple of days for people to make the connection between me and Jayson. Somehow people had figured out where I lived, and came by looking to catch a glimpse of Jayson or to ask questions about me. After one particularly scary encounter with a guy knocking on my door late one night, Jayson hired some security to sit outside my house. I had to give them a list of people who were allowed up to the house. After a couple days of that, the strangers stopped coming. Jayson had also made it clear via his social media that he was in Raleigh. There were still some people who wanted the personal details about me, but they didn't really bother me. I was thankful that they lost interest quickly. Ever since the end of the Series, Jayson had been incredibly busy with promotion, commercials, and team business, so we hadn't seen each other since he brought me home that night. We spoke every day, but I really wanted to have him in my bed for the night.

There just wasn't anything like having him next to me when I slept. He was safe, he was my home.

I was restless waiting for his call. I knew I needed to sleep because in just a few short hours I would be running the half-marathon that I had spent the last nine months training for. I think it was that first run that Jayson took with me that had me falling for him. He was as connected to this as I was. The last couple months hadn't been great for training with all of the travel, but I was still feeling good about what I was going to do. The only thing that would make it better was Jayson being here to share it with me. Unfortunately, he was stuck across the country shooting more ads for the shoe company that endorsed him. It is work, so I get it, but it didn't make it easier.

I tossed and turned most of the night, so when the alarm went off at three thirty, I was already awake. Before I showered, I went down to the basement to warm up a bit on the treadmill. After about thirty minutes, I was ready to get this thing in motion. I dressed in layers since it would be a cool start, and there was going to be almost an hour of standing around before we even got moving. All I had to do was get to the meeting spot, unload the jogger and wait.

By the time I got to the park where the race was to start, there were already hundreds of people gathered. I saw Cindy waiting patiently with Kenneth as I rolled up with the jogger. I worked to get him seated and covered up before I started on the electronics. I had set my phone to interrupt me when he used the speech-generating app on his iPad. He could watch his movies, but get my attention by cutting through my music as needed. We tested it out a few times, and then Cindy and I went over how she could follow our progress on her phone. She gave out the last few hugs, and we were off to find our starting corral. As we were getting lined up, my phone rang and I was thrilled to see it was Jayson calling.

We spoke for a few minutes as I stretched my legs and got ready to move. He wished me luck, and let me know to call him as soon as I was done. After I disconnected, I checked on Kenneth one more time to make sure he was ready to go. Before I knew it, the run had started, and we began creeping forward. There was a long loop to get out of the park, and for most of it, we were packed close. It wasn't until we were right on the edge of the park near the two-mile mark that the herd began to thin out. I was able to pick up my pace a bit and find a groove. Right as we approached the three-and-a-half-mile marker, I heard very loud cheering. I was surprised to see a few of the boys from my baseball team, as well as a few of my students and their parents there cheering us on. I definitely needed that boost.

I continued my steady pace as we approached a part of the course that I was not looking forward to. It was a mile-long stretch that was all uphill. This was something that I wish I had spent more time on. Of course, I had trained on an incline, but only a few of those sessions included me pushing the weight I was pushing now. I was able to keep my pace, and just as we started the climb, my playlist hit the songs that I needed to keep me going. I had loaded two songs by The Prodigy back-to-back, and if anyone can get you moving, it's them. Right at the top of the hill I heard that same loud cheering I heard before, and once again we were greeted by more members of my team, as well as more students. I tried to remain focused, because I had not quite hit the halfway point, but I swear, out of the corner of my eye, I caught a glimpse of Jayson near the back of the crowd with my mom. I'm sure it was wishful thinking on my part, so I didn't even look back.

Kenneth and I had just made the final turn on to the last mile-and-a-half straightaway when I started to lose step. I was completely spent. This was truly the hardest part of the race. Just as I was talking myself into quitting, Kenneth's voice came up in my headphones. He asked how much longer we had, and if he could listen to music. It was a very welcome distraction. My phone was paired with his iPad, so all he had to do was close out his apps to hear my music. I let him know we were just about there, and to be ready to get his medal. I peeked down to see a huge smile on his face. The park was finally in sight, and this was almost over. Hopefully my mom and Cindy would be waiting like I asked to take the jogger from me so I could cool down.

The minute I looked at the finish line, I saw him standing there with my mom. He was bundled in sweats and had a hat pulled down over his eyes. He had a blanket over his arm, as well as a medal in his hand. I made the final push, and just as we crossed, Cindy took the stroller and bent down to put the big medal on Kenneth. I needed to cool down, so I didn't stop right away. I knew if I did, I wouldn't be able to walk at all.

Jayson took up in a jog next to me, wrapping the blanket over my shoulders and asked, "How long do I have to chase you until I get my kiss?" I gave him the same answer I gave Mom when she asked how long it took me to cool down after the race, "One 'Bohemian Rhapsody'." Jayson kept pace with me as I slowed down to a walk. As soon as we were away from the crowds, I stopped, and he pulled me in for his hug and kiss. I was still in a bit of a shock from just having run over thirteen miles and I didn't even know what to say. I stood there looking at him, and there was something different that I couldn't quite put my finger on. Finally, Jayson gave me a smile and took his hat off. His long hair that he typically kept under his hat had been cut off. I didn't think it was possible for him to get any sexier, but I was dead wrong.

He ran his hand over the top and said, "They did it for this last commercial. I usually do it this time of year anyway, but I knew you liked it longer, so I wasn't going to cut it. Do you like it?" I looked up at him and smiled.

"I absolutely love it! I can't wait to see you in a suit with that haircut. Your tattoos peeking out at your wrists and collar." The thought sent a shiver right down my spine.

"Well, I guess it's a good thing I packed a few suits for my stay."

"Your stay?" I asked, hopeful.

"If you'll have me, I plan on staying until I have to go back to work. Of course, I figured we could squeeze a couple vacation days away in there. But otherwise, I told my agent I'm off until February."

Chapter 22

Everlong

Holiday time with my family was nothing short of a full-scale production. From shortly after Halloween, through the New Year, there would be decorations, parties, food, and LOTS of family time. While this is a regular part of my life, there was one thing that was going to be very new this year...Jayson. This was also going to be something very new to him. We had spoken a few times about the strained relationship he had with his family, but I thought the holidays would be different. I had brought up Jayson bringing his family out to meet me and my family, but he said a very solid no. He wanted to have a real family Christmas with no obligations. He was even more serious about the no-obligations part than the no-family part. Jayson didn't do any work other than exercise while he was here. I think he only talked to his agent once about a fundraiser in February. Otherwise, his attention was totally on me and my family.

***

I stood at the kitchen island preparing some of the things for Christmas Eve dinner when Jayson came up behind me. He wrapped his arms around my waist and leaned over to whisper in my ear. Just as I felt his lips touch my neck, I heard a throat clearing, so I looked up. My oldest sister Claire and her husband Roger had arrived.

"I was hoping this day would never come," Roger said, earning a slap on the shoulder from my sister.

She ungraciously said very loud, "You didn't expect her to be a single virgin forever, did you?"

Roger quickly retorted, "That's exactly what I expected! She's just a baby."

Laughing, Claire said, "Sweetheart, she is twenty-six years old. I'm sure she punched her v-card a long time ago!"

I was completely mortified that they were talking about me like that. And Jayson was just laughing quietly in my back. "You both realize that I am sanding right here. We are standing right here. And even if I wasn't, that shouldn't be a conversation that the two of you are having!"

"Cadie, you realize that I have known you most of your life. You are my little sister as much as you are Claire's. In my mind, you will always be that awkward eight-year-old little girl I met so long ago." Roger's words had me even more embarrassed.

All I could manage by way of a reply was, "I was not awkward!" They both started laughing instantly, which caught Jayson's attention.

He said, "Oh, I think I need to hear this story!"

To which my sister was more than happy to share.

"Let's see, how do I even explain this. Cadie is the very epitome of an ugly duckling. Growing up she was too skinny, with stringy hair, and God-awful teeth. Pops also tried to turn her into a tomboy, but that never really worked out. Roger and I started dating when I was seventeen, so that is the Cadie that he met. We went off to college, and Cadie got braces to fix her teeth and a shorter haircut to fix the stringy mess. Did I mention she also had really thick glasses? Because she did!" Claire was nearly doubled over in laughter at this point. She continued on with a bit more of a straight face, "Well, I finished school and came home for a summer visit only to see that Cadie got her braces off, got contacts, now had beautiful red hair, and that body! You can only imagine my surprise when in the three months it had been since Easter, my baby sister went from complete dork to pin-up model at age fourteen. Yes, she had the body she has now at fourteen! I think Roger had his first stroke then, seeing her like that. Luckily, we still lived up in Berkley because he wouldn't have been able to handle seeing young high school boys take her out. When we finally decided to come home, Cadie was headed off to college, and there wasn't much we could do with her in another state, so out of sight, out of mind, I guess."

"You were too young to really enjoy Vegas, so while you were there, I didn't really worry about you," Roger said. "I also know that student athletes are basically banned from the casinos and clubs, so that would keep you out of trouble." I couldn't help but laugh at that. It was true that student athletes all took a course on the dangers and ramifications of gambling as well as underage drinking. Not that it really stopped anyone.

"You know, Roger, even if I didn't hit the strip, every rental home in Vegas comes with a pole and a slot machine as standard furnishing. I couldn't escape it if I tried." My words seemed to cause his stomach to turn and his face to wrench. "Your ass had better not have slid down a pole in Vegas, or anywhere, for that matter!"

Jayson pressed his forehead between my shoulders to stifle another laugh, and he whispered, "I've got a friend with a pole in the basement."

I winked at him over my shoulder and said, "I know, it's me." Luckily, that officially ended the conversation and the remainder of the evening was pleasant.

The next morning, I sneaked downstairs to make sure that everything was perfect. The big tree, lots of presents, and of course, the stockings were all hung over the fireplace. After I saw that everything was in place, I made my way back upstairs to Jayson. He was snoring quietly as I pulled the covers back and slid back into bed. I loved the way his skin and tattoos looked against the bright white sheets. I couldn't help myself. I glided my fingers up his arm and over his chest. Without opening his eyes, he smiled wide and gripped my wrist, pulling me close. Big arms encircled me, and Jayson whispered softly, "Merry Christmas, my love. Are you ready to open your presents?"

I smiled into his chest and said, "It seems like the best gift I got this year doesn't really need to be unwrapped." I melted into Jayson as he pushed me over on my back, pressing me firmly to the mattress. Before I could even take a breath, his big hands were roaming down my sides to my thighs. He pulled one of my legs over his hip and buried himself deep inside of me. It was like second nature at this point. My body just naturally responded to him. Open-mouthed kisses heated my neck as Jayson worked my body to the breaking point. Just as I was about to call out, his mouth covered mine, swallowing my moan. I'm glad he remembered that there were guests downstairs because the only thing I could think about right now was how incredible this felt.

I never wanted to let him go, so we got in the shower together to get ready for the big reveal downstairs. Despite his initial protests, Jayson dressed in the matching pajamas that I had ordered for us. I can't even say that he looked silly in the striped bottoms and thermal top, despite the fact that the arms and shoulders looked ready to rip apart at any moment. As we made our way downstairs to the chatter-filled kitchen. The entire family was gathered making breakfast. Jayson took in the sight, and I could see him relax immediately. Every member of the family was wearing the same ridiculous outfit. Yep, we are that family. I'm sure if I didn't insist on it, it wouldn't happen, but since I'm the baby, they humor me.

I rush everyone through the food part of the morning because I am so excited to open gifts! I might be twenty-six, and I now understand that the holiday is about more than gifts, but it is still my absolute favorite part. Everyone in my family goes all out. Mom still follows her tradition of getting each person something they need, something to read, something to wear, and something they want. Claire and Roger always get everyone the exact same gift, usually whatever the hottest new gadget is. Katrina and Phillip just give cash. It's a good thing their sons have us, or else they would be the kids with no toys on Christmas. I spend the year doing recon and listening for any hints of what people really want. I try and find the perfect gift that also has a lot of sentimental value. Little humble brag on my part, but I always nail it. This year, I had to act fast when it came to Jayson. He had mentioned something to me when he first saw the Chevelle in my garage. Almost immediately, I began hunting down a 1967 Camaro. It's in rough shape, but my papa always told me the best part was putting in the work to fix it up. I hope Jayson feels the same way. The hardest part came in tracking down the miniature replica that is now resting in the bottom of his stocking serving as a placeholder. The real deal was delivered to his garage a couple days ago.

Open gifts filled the room along with mountains of paper and ribbon. Jayson had gifted me a week's vacation in Taha'a, French Polynesia. I've never even heard of it before, but we are leaving tomorrow! He assured me that everything is already taken care of; all I have to do is wake up and get dressed in the morning. Mom is sitting on a chair, smiling and fiddling with the new e-reader Jayson got her. She looked up for a minute and announced that it was time for stockings. Everything in them in always just fun stuff. They are filled with candy, and silly toys and games like slime and decks of cards. I watch intently as Jayson pulls the little car from his. He smiles wide and says, "You remembered." Of course, I remembered. Then, I lean over and tell him that there is a big-boy version parked in the garage at his house waiting for him to work on. His eyes go wide and he pulls me on to his lap. For a moment, it is just us two. This has been an amazing Christmas morning.

"Cadie, I've never had a holiday like this. Growing up my family didn't do things like this. I had no idea just how special this day could be. I would, however, like to make just one more memory." He reaches across me and dumps the contents of my stocking all over the floor. I had been so busy watching him that I hadn't taken out a thing. Then, I spot it. He shifts me off his lap and scoops up the small red leather box.

On bended knee, in front of my family, Jayson takes my hand and says, "My dearest Cadence. When I first saw you six months ago, I knew you were going to change my life. What I couldn't have imagined was the profound effect you have had on me as a man and as an athlete. Every day you challenge me to do better, be more, and live fully. I never understood the depth of love that a person could feel until I had yours. We aren't two halves making a whole, because you are nothing less than everything. Will you extend me the greatest honor and agree to be my wife?" As if he had timed it perfectly, as soon as he said wife, the box opened, revealing a radiant-cut diamond on a diamond-encrusted band. Tears filled my eyes and I was unable to form words. Jayson plucked the ring from the box and held it to my outstretched hand, not sliding it on until I said the word.

I finally took a breath and said, "Yes," in nothing more than a whisper. I couldn't even look down at how it looked on my hand as I was too busy looking right into Jayson's beautiful brown eyes.

My mom's soft sniffle finally broke my gaze. A small tear ran down her cheek as she stood and clapped her hands once. She took Jayson in a big hug and said something very quietly to him. In a move that was very unlike anything I had ever seen from Jayson, he kissed Mom on the cheek and said, "I love you too." My brothers and sisters were all offering their congratulations, and the rest of the day passed in a blur.

***

What can I even say about spending a week in French Polynesia? It was pure magic. We had a private bungalow that jutted out over the water. I hate to even call it a bungalow because it was easily two-thousand square feet. Besides the staff that attended to our every wish, we didn't even see other people. I can't even say if there were other people on the island. We got there on a water taxi that was just for Jayson and me. For an entire week I forgot about the outside world. We swam, ate, drank too much, danced under the stars, and made love until we couldn't move. Perfection, that is what it was. It wasn't until the final leg of our trip home that I even thought about what was going to happen next. I twisted my new ring around my finger. Partly because I was nervous, and the other part was because I still wasn't used to the size of it. Each time I did that, Jayson made a comment about it needing to be bigger. For me, it was perfect. Apparently, he had spoken with my mom in advance, and not only got her permission, but her advice on what I would like. The ring was beautiful, and just my taste. But he thinks someone of his status should have gone bigger.

He sees me fidgeting and says, "We can always change the stone out, love. Maybe put that one in a necklace?" I stop him immediately.

"Jayson, we have already had this discussion. This is the perfect ring for me. Too big, even. How in the world am I going to stuff my hand in a baseball glove with this huge rock on my finger?"

He brings my hand to his mouth, kissing my ring, and says, "It's a good thing you don't need to worry about that anymore."

There it is. The start of the conversation I had been avoiding for months. We needed to live together but walking away from my life here is so hard. So instead of talking about it, I deflected and said, "Let's just get through the fundraiser in February, and then we can figure out all of the logistics." Jayson just lets out a long breath, leaned his head back, and closed his eyes. I think that bought me some time, but I think I also just hurt his heart.

Chapter 23

Waves

It was the evening of the fundraiser and I was full of nerves. Every minor league team held a winter fundraiser, and this year Jayson was the big draw. I hadn't told Jayson that some of the proceeds would be benefiting our family charity. We started it not too long after my accident while I was doing rehabilitation. So many of the kids who were in there with me had been in accidents that caused loss of limb, and in many cases, paralysis. I saw how those kids wouldn't get to experience sports, or life, for that matter, the same. Everything in their life changed. My mom and I wanted to give them the opportunity to keep moving forward like I was. Adaptive equipment and private lessons could achieve that. That's where our charity came in.

After Jayson spoke, he joined my family for dinner. Conversation around our table was easy. Everyone was engaged in all of the various side discussions that were happening. Jayson was on my left, speaking to my mom, while he held my hand and absentmindedly twisted my ring with his thumb. I had been so engrossed in what Jayson was talking to my mom about, that I didn't even see Nate approach until I was too late. His hand was on my shoulder before I even registered what was happening. Jayson stood the moment I tensed up, and my mother's hand gently grasped his forearm.

"Jayson, son, sit down. You don't get up in the middle of dinner to take out the trash." Jayson hesitated to sit, but took the nod from my mother that everything was going to be just fine. Everyone within earshot was going to get a first-hand lesson in a verbal takedown. My mother continued to speak in a calm and clear voice, but her attention was now aimed solely at Nathan Serpa. "Please remove your hand from my daughter." He did as he was told but didn't back away. "Thank you for coming tonight, Mr. Serpa. I'm guessing that the reason you are here is because the work that All Access Sports means a great deal to you, and not because you wanted to further torment my daughter. I read somewhere that you sustained quite an injury while you were away. Perhaps that is the reason that this is the charity you choose to support. It seems quite lucky that you are still able to walk, doesn't it?" Mom didn't need an answer and just kept talking. "You were very fortunate in that instance. That good fortune might not continue if you keep harassing my daughter. It would be quite embarrassing for you if the circumstances surrounding that injury, as well as where it was sustained, became public. You have been quite lucky that your criminal record is sealed, and you have been allowed gainful employment. When you get in bed tonight, remember to thank God, and me, for that good fortune."

"I just wanted to apologize to Cadence. I never got the opportunity. I am truly sorry." Nate was speaking to my mother, but the words were meant for me.

"Cadence neither wants nor needs your pitiful apology. You aren't the least bit sorry for what you did. Even if you were, Cadie isn't the one you should be seeking forgiveness from. She has done quite well for herself despite everything you took from her. It would be best if you find someone else to make you feel better about the devastation that you caused because there is no forgiveness or sympathy here for you." Mom was even more stern, and her voice had gotten quite loud.

Realizing he had been dismissed, Nate made the right decision and quickly backed away from the table. The moment he was gone, I let out a long breath. I looked around the table and saw my sisters quietly conversing with their husbands as if nothing had happened. Jayson, on the other hand, was in complete shock. I hadn't registered the grip he had on my hand throughout the exchange until we made eye contact. My mother was quite pleased with herself, and to be honest, I was too. She dealt with the aftermath of everything much more than I did. She shielded me from much of it since I was a teenager. Mom spoke up again, and everyone at the table gave her their full attention. "I do not tolerate any disrespect to my family, blood or otherwise. While I can hope that the fool who made that mistake tonight has learned his lesson, I expect my sons to handle things with him from here on out in the off chance he hasn't," she said as she patted Jayson's arm. "Now let's all forget about this unfortunate event and enjoy the remainder of the evening. Dessert looks quite delicious."

Enjoying the remainder of the evening didn't really happen. Jayson was on edge and constantly scanning the room. I finally made him get up and escort me to the ladies' room. While he tried to follow me inside, I had him stand at the door. When I emerged a few minutes later, I was not prepared for what I saw. Jayson had Derrick pinned against the wall with his forearm against his neck. Derrick's face was red, and he was apologizing profusely. After placing my hand on his shoulder, Jayson turned to me and let Derrick go. He was furious, but spoke calmly to me. "You know this piece of shit was friends with Serpa? I heard the two of them talking right after you went inside. He was only trying to befriend you so that Serpa could get an apology in! He took it too far,

Cadie. I can't stand for this." Jayson was vibrating with anger.

I leaned in to hug his side and whispered, "Just let Mom handle it from here. There is no need for you to get caught up in this mess he made." Derrick smartly said nothing and walked away from us for the last time. We made our way back to the table to excuse ourselves for the evening. I quietly told Mom what went down, and she let me know she would speak to the right people.

As soon as we could break away from the last person who wanted to shake hands and take a picture with Jayson, we made a break for the car. Our remaining time together was very limited, and we wanted to enjoy each second of our alone time.

***

We only had this weekend left until Jayson left for spring training. He was going to essentially be moving to Florida for a month before the official start of the season. For the first few weeks of that, we couldn't even see each other. The team goes on a lockdown of sorts to focus and work on team building. Since I couldn't go, and I wasn't about to move to a new town to be alone for weeks on end, Jayson agreed that it would be best if I stayed back in California. He did, however, want me in Raleigh at the earliest possible moment. I would be there for a visit for sure, but the official move was going to have to wait until I was done with the school year.

That decision led to the first of many fights over the next few weeks. I had just landed in Raleigh for the weekend, and Jayson picked me up from the airport. "When is the rest of your stuff going to be delivered? Do you need me to get someone to help you with the boxes when they get here?" When I didn't answer right away, he shook his head at me. The ride to his house was more than just quiet. The silence was deadly. Jayson never reached over the console to hold my hand or fidget with my ring. I don't think he even turned my direction, other than to look for traffic.

Once inside, Jayson went straight to the media room. He sat down with his head in his hands. Without looking up, he said, "Were you even going to tell me you aren't moving here, or are you just going to keep putting it off? Think we can do this forever?" His voice began to raise as he stood. "You live three-fucking-thousand miles away from me! I come home to an empty fucking house every night and you are off with your friends and family. That's supposed to be for me, Cadie. I'm your fucking family now! I need you here!"

I was standing stock-still, too afraid to even breathe. This was not the man I knew. Deep down I know he wouldn't physically hurt me, but right now I was truly terrified. There is not one thing that I could say in this moment that would fix this problem, so I was going to choose to say nothing at all. Jayson's eyes turned cold and he was staring right through me. Not getting what he wanted from me, he turned to leave the room. On his way out, he took one of the many baseballs down from the shelf and hurled it at the opposite wall, leaving a baseball-size hole in his wake.

Chapter 24

Schism

I really hated what had been going on between Jayson and me these last few weeks. Being apart from one another was really hard. Every one of our conversations ended in hurtful words. I was just surviving on a day-by-day basis. But today was one of the days in my life that I needed to enjoy. Every four weeks I sat in the chair of one of my closest friends, and we talked while she worked her hair color magic. She was one of the only people in my life who knew that the red hair I wore so effortlessly didn't come naturally.

The minute I sat down Melanie knew something was off. I was lucky to have her, and I was also lucky that she was so good at her job as my hairdresser, and pseudo therapist, that the conversation I needed to have was just going to happen organically. Melanie asked about work and my family, and we effortlessly chatted until it was time to process the color, and that is usually when the heavy stuff came out. "Things have just been very difficult these last few weeks, Mel," I told her honestly. "Jayson had to report for spring training, and while I knew we couldn't spend a great deal of time together, I didn't know it would be this hard. Ever since we came back from our vacation, he has been really pressing me to move to Raleigh with him. More than anything I wanted to, but I didn't want to walk away from my life here, especially knowing that he was going to be gone so much these first few months of spring. I was hoping to be able to hold out until school was out, but it is just so hard." I was nearly crying at this point.

Melanie held my hand and told me I made the right choice in staying because being alone in a new city would only make me resent Jayson. She also told me that this was a conversation that I needed to be having with him. That was the difficult part. He never saw past my decision to not move. Every time I said no, he just got pissed, and then we didn't talk about it, or worse, he screamed at me for leaving him alone. Jayson never asked why I said no. I know it hurts, but I really wanted him to understand why. I mean, at this point, my mind is made up, and I will be moving there the second that school is out for the summer, but Jayson doesn't know that yet, because if my answer isn't me on the next plane, he doesn't want to hear it.

I felt better not only physically but emotionally after leaving Melanie's. That feeling was short lived because as soon as I got in the car, Jayson called. He was on the road today, and I didn't remember exactly what city he was in. It's hard to memorize a schedule when there are well over one-hundred-and-fifty regular season games to play. He was in one city for a few days and then on to the next. It just worked out that this year he would be "home" during my spring break. As with all my breaks from school, I would be leaving immediately after work and staying until the last possible minute. This meant that for the first time in my life, I wasn't going to be with my mom for the holiday, but she understood.

I was right in the middle of telling Jayson about how it was going to be strange for me to be away from my mom for Easter since I hadn't done that before when he completely blew up. "Am I not family enough for you, Cadence? Why won't you just let it go. You should be here in my house with me, end of story." Of course, when I should have been understanding, I went the opposite route. "So, I just need to leave everything I know and wait around for you in YOUR house like a guest? Yeah, it's pretty clear that you don't really want me with you full time because it's still YOUR house and not OUR house. Not once since you came home after the Series did I call the house here in California, MY house. It was OURS then, and it still is. Maybe if Raleigh felt like home, I would be happy to be there."

I think I could feel the heat in his voice as he roared, "I can't make a home with you if you won't even give me the chance to. This is all on you, Cadie. You know you are afraid, even though I have done absolutely everything in my power to shield you from the world out there. Stop fucking being afraid of what everyone else says or does, and do what is best for me and you. When you are ready to do that, you know where you can find me." Then, the line went dead.

No "I love you."
No "goodnight."
Just silence.
Well-deserved silence.

Chapter 25

The Mixed Tape

After the fight that Jayson and I had on the phone last night, I decided that I would put off my trip to see him for a couple days so he could cool off. He has been constantly pressuring me to walk away from my life here in California to be with him full time. And each time the conversation turns into a shouting match. I have shown him over and over again that I have a life here full of commitments that I can't just walk away from, especially when he himself hasn't been home for two months. I also think I have done an amazing job of showing him just how flexible I am willing to be. Every possible day off I have, I spend it with him. Sleep and self-care have more than taken a back seat to making sure we spend as much physical time with one another as possible. Can't he give me just a couple more months, and then he will get what he wants? Of course, I haven't told him that yet, but I want to do it for us, and not just him.

I was exhausted after a very long day filled with two meetings, a full day in class, as well as a baseball game of my own to coach. I finally got home close to six, and while I should be headed to the airport, I was collecting the front porch deliveries. Another massive bouquet of the lavender roses were waiting on my step, as well as the ever-present Amazon boxes. I bring everything in and set them on the kitchen counter before collapsing on the couch. I hadn't heard from Jayson all day, which was unusual, but after the fight we had, it was expected. That's when I remembered my phone had died at my game, so I plugged it in and kicked my feet up. I flipped on the TV, and it just so happened that the sports report for the evening had just started. I watched mindlessly until the mention of Jayson snapped me back to reality. Once again, Jayson had been infuriated during the game. This time it was because he was hit by a pitch. It was obvious that it had been on purpose and Jayson was wired. When he got wired, he got careless, and that is the next clip they showed. A batter rounded third at full speed. Jayson flipped his mask off, and a second later they collided. I swear it happened in slow motion. My ears began to ring and I felt hot. The sudden blast of incoming texts from my phone powering back on brought me back to the present. As I held my phone, it began to ring.

"Cadence, are you there? Tell me you are at the airport and can get on a new flight. Where have you been? We have been trying to get in touch with you for almost two hours!" Sarena was talking so fast, I could barely register what she was saying. I was in shock.

"I'm at home," was I all could manage to squeak out before she started barking orders at me. She had arranged for a private flight to take me straight to Raleigh. There was now a car on the way to pick me up. Is Jayson going to be all right? What did I miss her saying to me? I shake the thoughts from my head and make my way over to the bouquet on my kitchen counter. I plucked the card from the center of the arrangement, and with one more deep breath I stepped outside, locked the door, and got in the car waiting at the curb.

Suddenly, the images from the television flashed in my mind. Jayson took the full force of the collision with the runner. He fell back and his head hit the ground hard. He stopped moving. He laid there motionless for what seemed like an eternity surrounded by coaches and trainers. Even when he got put on the gurney, he didn't move. There was no raised hand to the crowd as he was wheeled off. With that realization, that's when the first tear fell.

I held the notecard tight in my hand as I rode to the airport. I was getting on a private flight that would get me to Raleigh only about ninety minutes before I typically arrive. Sarena assured me that she would be waiting to collect me. All I could do was be patient. Through the tears I read the words that were on the notecard I had been clutching tight.

My Beautiful Cadence,

Music tells the stories that cannot be captured by words alone. There are so many times that I don't have the words that I need to tell you everything that I am feeling. These songs say everything that I have never been able to find the words for. Each song will tell you exactly what I have been feeling for you for the last nine months. This is our story from my side. I want you; I need you; I love you.

~Jayson

As I climbed the short staircase to the plane, I scanned the code that was on the backside of the note Jayson had sent with the flowers, and a playlist downloaded to my phone. I sat back in one of the oversized chairs, put my headphones in, and pressed play before the plane even started to roll. I listened to all the words that spilled out through the music for the next two hours. Tears rolled down my cheeks as I listened to songs that said all the things that Jayson showed me every day that we were together. They told our story from the moment we met. I should have never kept my full self from him. After our New Year's on the islands, I should have just gone "home." I can only hope that it won't be too late when I do get there. I do know that I'm never leaving. From now on, wherever Jayson is, that's my home.

Sarena had the engine running as I exited the doors of the airport. She had circled a few times waiting for me. As I settled in the seat next to her, she grabbed my hand and said, "You were the first and only person he asked for when he woke up. He needs you right now, Cadie, more than you could possibly know."

I got myself together enough so that I wouldn't make a scene rushing into the hospital. I stepped out into the crisp morning air and rushed toward the doors. I raced to the information desk and asked for Jayson. The clerk eyed me cautiously, not wanting to give up any information on where he might be. Pulling out the piece of paper that I had carried with me for months now, I placed it on the desk and said, "Please, ma'am, my name is Cadence Martinez and Jayson is my husband."

I had finally said the words out loud. There was no going back now. That's when I knew that another collision is what brought me home.

Jayson's Playlist on Spotify

Not on Spotify? The chapter names are the titles of the songs on Jayson's playlist for Cadie.

About the Author

Callie Sommers is the pen name that I have created to tell the many stories that have been swimming around in my head for the past 15+ years. I don't think of myself as a writer in any particular genre as I am figuring it out as I go. All of my writing is about human relationships. I love to figure out what makes people tick, and I want that to come out in my writing. I want my readers to know and love my characters as much as I do.

My mom taught me to read at a very young age and I have been devouring books ever since. I try and read one book every day. There are so many books that I call favorites, but Midnight In The Garden of Good and Evil by John Berendt is the book that made me fall in love with writing. So, I suppose his "non-fiction novel" style is what I pattern my own writing after. Every good novel is grown from a kernel of truth.

Want to know more about me? Feel free to ask, or give my books a read. They tell more than I ever will.

Facebook ~ @AuthorCallieSommers
Instagram ~ @calliesommers
Twitter ~ @sommers_callie
Website ~ www.calliesommers.com

Here are the first few chapters of the "Blog Novel" I'm am adding exclusively to my website.

Booker and Ace have been friends for years. This is how it all began.

Chapter 1 –

"Tonight is the night, Bar patrons! We are kicking off early to get to our party. That's right, after 15 years on air here in the Valley, Booker's Bar is going national. Starting Monday, people in 21 major cities all over the good ole' U.S. of A will be able to pull up a seat and have a stiff one with us. So, let's go celebrate at The Office. It also happens to be amateur night, so there will be plenty of nice young ladies looking to start their lifelong career of paying their way through school. Maybe we can finally get Ace up on that pole? What do you say Ace?"

"Sorry to disappoint everyone but I'm no amateur. I've been getting paid to have a creep stare at by boobs for ten years now, and I actually finished college. And ladies, Booker might park his ass on the tip rail but don't expect much. He's been sitting 3 feet from me all this time and I couldn't' even tell you what color his wallet is."

"You don't have to pay for the party, when you are the party Ace! Anyway, get out there friends and Ace and I will see you soon. Enjoy this next one on us! Cheers."

As soon as we are clear, Booker shakes his head and laughs at me. "Can you believe it had been ten years already? I am so proud of how far you have come. Maybe now you will think about settling down? While your horrific dating life makes for great radio, I want to see you settled and happy. You will always be my family, but you need to grow your branch of the tree."

Booker was right in so many ways. My dating life does make for fantastically entertaining radio, I should think about settling down, and Booker is the only real family I have. He has been my everything since I was just a kid. I met Booker when my life was in ruins and he helped me to rebuild. I will forever be in his debt for all that he has done for me.

Meeting Booker for the first time is burned into my brain. I knew him by reputation before I actually met him. He is a local celebrity after all. Booker is the King of the Late Night on the local alternative rock station. He was loud, crude, and hated as much as he was loved by everyone that could hear his voice. Making a scene was what he lived for. The wilder the situation the better. There was always someone trying to get him fired for the last offensive thing he did or said. This is precisely why I wanted to stay as far away from him as possible.

I started working at the station just six weeks after my mom unexpectedly passed away. One day she was there, and the next day she was gone. The final report said that she had an aneurysm. All I know is that the only family I knew was gone. My father was still alive, but he lived a few hours away and we hadn't had any sort of relationship in years. When I called him to let him know what happened, he was surprisingly kind. He helped me to make all of the arrangements and even helped with the seemingly endless paperwork stuff that a minor couldn't manage.

After the dust settled a bit, dad sat me down and asked what I wanted to do. He offered to move me in with him, but if was being honest he was a stranger, and the thought of leaving my friends and school behind with one year to go wasn't at all appealing. He agreed to let me stay put. The house was paid for with mom's life insurance money and there was some money in the bank to pay monthly bills, but it wouldn't last forever. I'd be turning eighteen in a few months and then I'd really be on my own. I started looking for a job that would be flexible without too much stress. The first job I applied for was an office assistant and I got it.

On my first day I was delivering the mail to the various offices when I nearly crashed right in to the infamous Booker. Clearly annoyed that I was even in the same hallway as him he barked out, "what's your name?" My eyes were wide and my throat was dry. Pissing this guy off could mean my job. "You can call me Elliott." His eyes were studying me very intently. "I asked what your name was. Once you tell me that, I will decide what to call you." Wow, was this guy serious? He was the jerk that everyone says he is.

In nothing more than a whisper I said, "Annalise, my name is Annalise." "Nope, full government name. What's it say on your driver's license if you are even old enough to have one?" Booker was teasing me now, and I relaxed a bit. "My name is Annalise Cordelia Elliott, but everyone just calls me Elliott and yes I'm old enough for a driver's license."

"Alright then Ace, let's dump the rest of that in this office here" he said opening the door we were standing outside and taking the mail from my hands. "You work for me now so no more mail, only fun shit. Let's go to my office and then we can discuss what happens next." I froze right where I stood. Now that he knows I am at least old enough to drive he expects me to have sex with him in his office? No way! I need to get out of here. I could feel myself inching away. "Ace, I'm not trying to fuck you. You are way too young for me or for sex for that matter. Get that shit out of your head. I just think you could use some fun in your life, and if you weren't aware, I am the King of good times. I'll talk to Robert and let him know of the change. Now let's get moving, we are on air in an hour."

I sat nervously in Booker's massive office. I'm fairly certain it took up half of the floor. There was a sectional sofa, recliner, massive TV in addition to the desk and office chairs. He was a big deal around here for sure. Booker moved to sit opposite of me at his desk. With his fingers steepled at his mouth he asked what brought me here. For the first time ever, I was able to talk about my mom without crying. "So, you are just seventeen and you live by yourself? Christ, please tell me I'm one of the only people that knows that. That is seriously dangerous. You aren't even a legal adult! What if something happens to you?" It was weird that he seemed more concerned about my situation than my own father. I was getting a bit worried that he might tell someone about what was going on and I'd have to go live with my dad or even worse go into the system for a few months. I let him know that I turn 18 in just a few months and would be out on my own anyway, this saves me some moves.

"Alright, well I'm going to be looking out for you from now on. My wife is going to kill me for letting you live alone, but I think if you promise to have dinner with us and let her fuss over you we will both survive this." The look of shock must have been painted in neon all over my face. Did he say he has a wife? The same guy that hosts amateur night at the strip club and guesses what color panties the female callers are wearing? Booker just starts laughing. "Yeah, I know, big shock huh? Yes, I am very happily married. Have been for nearly 10 years. But that is our little secret okay. I'm not sure anyone that works here even knows. We both prefer it that way. You will meet her this weekend. Now on to work stuff."

The next 30 minutes were a crash course in all things radio. Booker showed me his studio and went over some basic stuff about answering the phone and how the computer works. He just kept stressing that I will learn as we go and not to panic. Honestly, I wasn't even sure what I was going to really do. I guess I will answer the phone and let him know who is calling. Maybe get him something to drink or open his mail. "I got you" seemed to be the summation of my job description.

Booker pointed to the chair across from him and told me to have a seat. He handed me a box with some new headphones with instructions to hurry up and plug in. I fumbled a bit with the packaging as I pulled out a pair of very expensive pink headphones. I plugged them in just as he started talking. "Good evening patrons and welcome to Booker's Bar. We have a brand-new special tonight and she goes by the name of Ace. I can't wait for all of you to get a good look at her! Hey Ace, say hello to the good people and tell them when your birthday is." He mouthed, "just talk to me." I swallowed hard and said, "hey everyone, I'm Ace and my birthday is October 17th. Wait, why did you need to know my birthday?" This is where the Booker we all knew came out.

"After some quick calculations, I am happy to say that it is a short 84 days until Ace here is legal. The countdown will be up on my page shortly. Until then fellas and maybe some of you ladies, keep it to yourself and avoid the bookings! How about a little Criminal by Fiona Apple to set the tone?" The song started to play and I stared wide eyed at Booker half wanting to cry and half wanting to slap him.

"Annalise, you have absolutely nothing to worry about with me. This is all a bit for the show. It's a joke and it is going to get the exact kind of reaction I want to get more people tuning in. You'll see it's all fun." My mind wasn't set at ease at all. In fact, I was horrified and mortified.

"Booker, you do realize that I am still in high school and that many of my peers are you biggest fans. In two weeks, I have to go back there! They might not know my voice on the radio, but you put my picture up and they will know for sure. I'm going to get harassed or even worse expelled!" The tears were falling, but the song was almost over and it was go time again. As the last few notes played Booker looked at me will all sincerity and said, "I fix this. You'll see. We are going to be the next big thing." And with a wink Booker was back and taking calls.

Chapter 2 – A Simple Plan

As promised, Booker "fixed" things. Not really fixed, more like diverted attention. Almost immediately people started calling in saying awful things about Booker or saying filthy things to me. The professional that he is handled everything.

He made jokes, turned people's words around on them, and thanked them for listening. It was really quite amazing how many people that hated him not only listened to the show, but called in to talk to him. I guess that is why he is who he is. Still don't know what I am doing here, but I am getting the hang of it.

By the end of the week, I am answering calls and putting them in the que. I'm also talking a lot more than I thought I was going to. Of course, Booker is always catching me off guard when he says something to me. It wasn't long before I realized that he does it to get an honest reaction from me. Authenticity makes for good radio. There is no script, just some general ideas about what the show is going to be about. Those general ideas always include, alcohol, strippers, panties, and embarrassing me. The first three things were the usual topics that fueled the fourth.

I also spent some time with Booker's wife during those first two weeks working for him. Let me say she wasn't at all who I would have expected to be married to a guy like Booker. Though, I have quickly realized that he isn't the guy that he wants everyone to think he is. Emma is quiet, sweet, and a little conservative. She was incredibly kind to me when we met, cooking dinner and making sure that I had food at my house to feed myself. She even asked me if she could take me "back to school" shopping. While my budget didn't allow for too much, it was a good trip none the less. We walked around the mall and talked about everything and nothing. It was like having a fun older sister and mom all rolled into one. There were a couple times where I completely broke down in a store, and Emma just hugged me and let me cry. She never made me feel like it was too much for her even though I could barely stand up under the weight of the situation. "I wish you were old enough to have a drink with," Emma said with sincerity. "There isn't a problem in the world that can't be made a little better with the help of Jose Cuervo. But Booker would kill me if I 'contributed to the delinquency of a minor.' His words not mine. You know he already thinks of you as the little sister he never had. Anyway, back to shopping. Booker said that I need to make sure you have notebooks and pens and 'all that school shit' before we head home." She had used air quotes a few times during her tangent and I couldn't help but laugh at her and Booker. We hit a big box store for all the school goods before dinner at home with Booker.

After spending the day with Emma, I finally felt comfortable enough to ask the question that had been bugging me since we first met. "How do you manage to keep the Booker that everyone knows so separate from your regular life? Can you guys even go out on dates without being bothered? I'm sure he has to be "Booker" out in public all the time, right?" She wiped her hands on the dishtowel and told me the story. She and Booker have basically been together since they were kids. They got married as soon as she turned 18 and they moved out west. They were so used to being homebodies having been so broke those first few years while they were in college, they just kept it up once his show hit. Now, when they want to get away, they really get away. Otherwise, they are perfectly happy just being home and being themselves. It was really sweet and I could tell their bond was strong.

#

"Our End of Summer Backyard BBQ is tomorrow at the fairgrounds and you all better be there! If the stellar line-up that is going to be taking the stage isn't enough to get you to open up your wallet for tickets, our very own Ace will be making her public debut. So, get those cards out and buy what few tickets are left, because you don't want to be the one waiting at the gate when we sell out!"

Every time he mentioned this big concert, the phones began to ring. Most people just wanted free tickets, while others wanted information on me. They asked things like my hair and eye color, while others asked things that were far more inappropriate. Just like he always did, Booker handled the more aggressive callers with his usual assholery. When one caller crudely asked how big my "tits" were, he told him "They aren't as big as yours so you don't need to feel competitive."

Booker could tell almost immediately that it all was making me uncomfortable. During one of the breaks, we came up with a plan for the day. I was to stay away from him and hang out with his wife. Apparently, she didn't get to go to these things very often and this way we could both enjoy it. He would wait for just the right moment to introduce me and then make sure I go out of the venue safe and without a tail.

The next day Emma came over bright and early to help me get ready, though I'm not sure why. By the end of the night, I was going to be a sweaty exhausted mess. What the real purpose of this early morning mission was to make sure that I was dressed appropriately. The shorts I was wearing when I answered the door were "too short" and my shirt "just wasn't right." I wasn't sure what else to wear, and that's when I noticed the shopping bag Emma had with her. "I took the liberty of bringing you a few things for the day. You can be comfy and then change right before showtime" she said as she pulled a few things out and put them on the bed. "I'm thinking the skirt and station shirt for the introduction but for the rest of the day you can look a bit more like me." Simple ripped jeans and a plain black tank was something I might have picked for myself if it weren't going to be so hot. As if she had read my thoughts she said, "we have passes to the VIP area and there is shade, cold drinks, and a non-public bathroom so you aren't going to melt or pass out. The people at the station already know you, so it won't be odd that you are there and for all intents and purposes you are my sister. We are all good."

Emma and I said a passing hello to Booker when we first arrived, but otherwise we stayed clear of him. The day had really passed in a blur. I hadn't had fun like this is quite a while. At least for today I was able to feel like a teenager enjoying the last bit of summer. That was all going to be ending very shortly. My senior year of high school was going to be starting in five days, but first my identity was going to be revealed to the masses and the last bit of normalcy in my life would be gone. But really, things hadn't been normal in months. There wasn't anybody I knew of in my position. I needed to let that go and just enjoy myself.

I sat on the grass and chatted with Emma as the first "big name band" took the stage. That brought a bunch more people to the area to watch the show. It wasn't that big of deal when someone came and sat nearly next to us. I looked over and saw a guy that had to be close to me in age, but wasn't anyone that I recognized from work. He wore khaki shorts and a black tee that said "role model" on the front with his Vans and his socks pulled up too high. Your typical skater kid uniform. His dark hair was styled in that way that made it look like he didn't try too hard, but had actually spent an hour on it. Maybe he was one of the college interns that I hadn't met yet? Didn't think much of it and went back to enjoy the music.

The music was loud, but I had earplugs in that helped filter out the "noise." I wouldn't have even turned towards him when he asked, "do one of your parent's work for the people putting this thing on," except I could feel his breath on my neck. The guy that had sat too close just a few minutes ago was now a bit too close for comfort. I leaned away and didn't respond right away. I had to take a deep breath and swallow the tears down because I immediately thought about my mom. I just shook my head and flashed my staff pass. Emma must have heard what he asked and she patted my back. That did it. The tears immediately began to fall. I tried really hard to get them to stop, but they wouldn't.

"I didn't mean to upset you princess. I just couldn't think of a better opening line." Mystery guy sounded apologetic, but I just wasn't able to say anything. Luckily, Emma had my back and was offering me a hand to stand up and move before more tears came. She looked to him and tilted her head knowingly. "It's been a bit of a rough summer for Ace, she'll be fine. Just not in the mood to talk right now. We also have to go get changed. See you around." As we walked away he said, "Princess, I will find you later and I want a do-over." I gave a simple nod and Emma walked me toward the lounge where I would get changed.

Emma spent nearly an hour working some sort of voodoo on me that made it look like I hadn't just spent the last 6 hours at a music festival. The denim skirt she had chosen hung just low enough on my hips to let a small sliver of my stomach show beneath the shirt she created. She had taken one the regular station tees and turned it in to an off the shoulder show stopper. I looked much older now, which was apparently what Booker had requested. This way people would see the birthday countdown and everything else as a big joke. He really did know how to play the game. We were making our way back outside when Emma stops me to say, "I'm going to leave right after you are introduced, so I won't see you until lunch tomorrow. Have a goodtime out there and trust Booker." One more hug and I was off.

I stood next to Booker as the last of the equipment was loaded and set in place. My nerves were starting to take over and I'm pretty sure I began to shake. Calmly Booker placed a hand on my shoulder and said, "you know everything is going to change, but be fine all at the same time, right? I wouldn't be doing any of this if I wasn't 100% sure that it was the best move. I'm going to head out and then you will follow. You don't have to say a word, just wave and take it in." With those few words he walked onstage to the roar of the crowd. I was so transfixed by the sound that I almost missed him say my name.

I took a few cautious steps on stage and it was so loud and so bright that I could barely get my feet to move. I did manage enough sense to wave to the crowd of people I couldn't see as I moved across the stage. Booker said a few more things I couldn't understand and then the lights went down. I felt his hand on my shoulder as he walked me back to our seats on the side of the stage. "See, that wasn't so bad. You did good kid. Now, we get you out of here safely and by morning we will be all over…" Booker was cut off by the same voice that I heard earlier, the one that made me cry. Except this time, it was amplified for the entire amphitheater to hear. "Hey Princess, if I embarrass myself by asking you out in front of 20,000 thousand people will that make up for my terrible first impression? What do you say? Booker, help me out here. Have dinner with me princess. I'm not starting the show until you say yes." I was frozen. That guy that tried talking to me is the lead singer for the headlining band? I know Booker said things were going to change, but this? This isn't real. My thoughts were interrupted by, "you are leaving me and all of these people waiting princess, what do you say?" Since I had been rendered speechless, the only thing I could do was nod "yes." No longer a mystery man pumped his fist in the air and strummed the first chord of a song I was very familiar with.

"I guess sneaking you out of here on a tour bus will be a lot easier than my plan of hiding you in the station van" Booker shouted over a laugh. "I'm going to have a nice long conversation with that young man before you guys go anywhere." With one more pat on my shoulder Booker reminded me that everything was going to change. Boy was that an understatement. My first date ever was going to be with the lead singer of one of the biggest bands on the radio. He does know I'm only 17, right?

(Read the rest on: www.calliesommers.com)